SMASH

HARD HIT #14

CHARITY PARKERSON

--Warning: This book is intended for readers over the age of 18.

Copyright © 2018 Charity Parkerson
Editor: Hercules Editing & Consultants
ISBN: **ISBN-13: 978-1-946099-40-2**
All rights reserved.

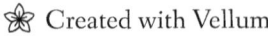 Created with Vellum

INTRODUCTION

KENTUCKY ALREADY LOST HIS CAREER ONCE. HE
THOUGHT REGAINING IT MEANT EVERYTHING.
UNTIL HE MET RORY.

After getting picked up by New York, getting injured, and let go, Kentucky is back in Texas. Working at his dad's auto repair shop isn't terrible, but it's not his dream. He needs ice under his skates. Kentucky hasn't given up. He's determined to reclaim the career he loves. That is, until he meets Rory.

Rory recognized Kentucky the first time he laid eyes on him. That's not why he set out to win him. Kentucky has sad eyes Rory can't resist. He only wanted to know him. Rory never expects to love him. He doubly never intends to ruin Kentucky.

It's so easy for Kentucky to fall for Rory. The man is perfect in every way. Except Rory has a secret that could smash Kentucky's life to bits. Kentucky will have to decide what he can live with and who he can't live without.

ONE

AFTER A WINTER LIVING IN NEW YORK, Kentucky couldn't decide if a Texas summer was welcome or hell. There was a guy staring at him. Kentucky tried avoiding eye contact. Things always started the same way. Someone would stare, trying to decide if he was that one hockey player. Eventually, they always worked up the nerve to ask, and then Kentucky had to spend ten minutes of his life reliving the loss of his greatest dream. He'd made it to the big time for like five minutes. In truth, it was for five games. After years of grinding in the minors, Kentucky had finally been picked up by a major team. He'd hoped for at least one season on the ice in New York. Five games in, he tore out his knee and went down for the season.

Now, here he was, back in Texas and fixing cars in his dad's shop. It was an honest living. Kentucky rubbed his chest. This wasn't the dream he'd had for himself.

"Rory Vega. You're good to go," Kentucky called, ready to hand over the car he'd just finished to its owner. No one liked waiting for an oil change. Kentucky felt the man's approach, but he didn't look up from the paperwork he needed to initial. "You'll probably need a new air filter the next time you come in. I topped off your windshield wiper fluid and your left front tire was a little low. It's all good now."

"You're going to think this is an odd question," Rory said, interrupting him.

Kentucky glanced up, finding the dark eyes that had been watching him now holding his gaze. A smile tugged at Kentucky's lips. If he'd realized his stranger was so freaking hot, he would've made more of an effort to meet the guy's stare. "Odd is my middle name." Kentucky winked. "Not really. It's Scott. What is it I can do for you?" Even though losing his career was the worst thing to ever happen to him, he wasn't above using that minute of fame to land a hot piece of ass.

To his surprise, Rory's staring had nothing to do

with hockey. "Were you at Albott's grocery on Main last night around seven?"

Kentucky blinked. "Uh. Yeah."

The dude's smile was amazing. It was deep lines that proved he did it often. Damn, coupling that with the perfect runner's build, dark hair, and caramel skin... wow. "I thought you looked familiar. I was behind you in line."

He was right. That was an odd detail to remember. "It's a small world, I guess."

Rory shrugged. "Normally, I don't think I'd remember something like that, but we were in line forever. Also, you had jarred spaghetti sauce, and I was pitying you."

A smile tugged at the corners of Kentucky's mouth. "Yeah. I'm not a cook." He tore off the man's copy of the paperwork.

Rory didn't reach for it. "Did you write your number on there?"

Kentucky didn't respond. In truth, he didn't know how to react. He was usually the flirt.

The guy's smile hitched up a notch. "You know, so I can make you a real meal."

"Hey, Kentucky, I need you to pull the blue Toyota into bay four."

Kentucky glanced his dad's way. "Yes, sir. I'm on it."

"Oh well. Another time, I guess." That was all the warning Rory gave before he took the papers from Kentucky and slid behind the wheel.

Before Kentucky had time to recover, he'd lost his chance. Rory was already pulling away. Well, fuck. His shit luck held true. Another good thing slipped through his fingers.

GOOSEBUMPS ROSE on Rory's skin as another chill washed over him. He hated the cold. This was why he lived in Texas. Plus, everyone he'd met during his years living in California had been fake as hell. He was much happier here. Rory loved to skate as much as the next person, but damn Old West Ice kept it beyond fucking freezing in their rink.

"Tell me again why you forced us to join you in this upcoming disaster," Jay said, sounding bored.

Rory looked away from searching for his prey long enough to focus on Jay. His hands were encased in fingerless gloves and wrapped around a cup of hot chocolate. Everything about the man screamed runway from his dark, on point hair, painted nails, and glittery outfit. Lucas was no better. His blond hair was a mess, but he'd worn his fur coat. Rory barely stopped himself from rolling his eyes. He did a lot of stupid shit for them. They could do this for him.

"Because," Rory said, sounding exactly like he'd already explained this ten times, because he had. "While charming the woman who works the front counter at Armhill Auto, she told me Kentucky would be here tonight."

Lucas popped his gum. "I don't understand why you're doing this. You should've just grabbed his ass at the grocery store, told him you're a fan from his hockey days, and fucked him. He'd come back for more."

"Shhh." Rory shot a look around. "There're kids here."

Lucas rolled his eyes. The childish gesture did nothing to take away from his beautiful green gaze.

Jay jumped in. "Lucas is right. You're better than this."

A sigh came from Rory's soul and left his lips. "If a fan approached you, wanting to take you home, how would you react?"

A scandalized look passed over his face. "Um, first of all, the whole world knows I'm with Lucas."

The pair blew each other a kiss. "Second of all... I see your point. This is better. Still, how did you convince her to tell you where he'd be?"

Rory shrugged. "I simply asked if she thought he'd go out with me tonight. She told me she doubted it. His baby brother has a birthday party here tonight, and no way would Kentucky miss it."

A snort escaped Lucas. "You should've just asked him out for tomorrow night. Damn, you've already gotten an unnecessary oil change over this. For that matter, Jay is right; you should've approached him at the store. Instead, you sneaked a peek at the name on his work shirt and decided to stalk him like a crazy person."

"I am a crazy person," Rory said absently as he eyed the crowd.

"Be that as it may, he's right over there," Jay said, nodding to the left.

Rory followed his chin. Kentucky held a little boy's hand, skating slow and protecting him from being run over by bigger and faster people. He took a deep breath. "Wish me luck." Rory flashed them a warning look. "And don't leave yet. If I get shot down, I don't want to limp out of here alone."

"We'll be here."

"Go get him, tiger," Lucas called as he skated away.

Another sigh escaped him. Jesus. If he didn't love them so much... His nerves were already bad. Rory was naturally an over-confident person, but this was insane, even for him. When he'd spotted the ex pro hockey player in line ahead of him the night before, he'd been wowed. It was a matter of pride for him to know all the names of the out and proud players in professional sports. He'd never expected the man to be so hot in person. The impact had left Rory speechless, especially the man's eyes. He looked sad. Rory hadn't expected that either. By the time he'd found his courage at the store, he'd lost his chance. Now here he was, three steps into the craziest fucking plan he'd ever concocted, which was saying a lot. In for a penny. He pasted on a huge smile.

Kentucky stopped skating and went down on his haunches. Damn, the guy had an amazing ass. And that long, thick blond hair... yum. Rory wanted to bury his fingers in it. He skated in close. "Okay. Now it's more than just uncanny. It's kismet."

Kentucky turned from where he was zipping the little blond boy's jacket. A bright smile lit his face, stealing Rory's breath. "Are you sure you're not simply stalking me?"

The remark hit home. Rory fought to keep an innocent smile in place. "I'm just lucky, I think."

Kentucky stood. He held the boy's hand while offering his free one to Rory. "I'm Kentucky."

"Rory," Rory said, shaking his hand.

"I remember." The way Kentucky said those two words had butterflies stirring in Rory's stomach.

Rory motioned toward the boy. "And you are?"

"This is my brother, Lexi. We're here celebrating his fourth birthday."

"Four," Rory exclaimed as if it was the biggest number he'd ever heard. "No way. You're getting so old. You'll have wrinkles soon." Rory switched his attention back to Kentucky. "I'm sorry. I didn't mean to interrupt your party."

"We have cake," Lexi said, dragging Rory's attention back his way. "It's brown."

"He means chocolate," Kentucky said with a chuckle. It was hot.

Lexi nodded. "And trucks."

Rory lifted his eyebrows in question.

Kentucky smiled. "His presents have trucks on the wrapping paper."

"Ah. This sounds like an amazing party. I'm super jealous."

"You can come if you want."

At Lexi's invite, Rory glanced Kentucky's way again. He wasn't sure how to react. "I'm sure your family—"

"Would be thrilled," Kentucky said, interrupting him. "Trust me."

Still, Rory wasn't sure. He'd come here to accidentally on purpose see Kentucky, but he'd had no plans to crash a kid's party. "Um."

"You should join us," Kentucky said, cutting off his excuse before he found one.

Rory glanced behind him, making sure Lucas and Jay were still waiting. They were. He met Kentucky's stare once more. "Sure. Just give me ten minutes to find my friends and I'll be there."

Kentucky's smile brightened. "We're in the party room by the game room. I'll see you in ten."

Rory nodded before focusing on Lexi once more. "I want to hear all about the trucks."

"Dear God," Kentucky breathed. "You've done it now."

With a laugh, Rory skated backward. "See you in ten." Without waiting for a response, he skated away. Maybe he should, but Rory didn't feel the least bit guilty for chasing a man he didn't know. He had so few chances to meet nice men.

AS KENTUCKY WATCHED Rory skate away, he wondered if he'd really show. He couldn't imagine someone as sexy as Rory having nothing better to do than come to a kid's birthday party, especially one he didn't know. With a shake of his head, he helped Lexi skate back toward the party room. He should probably let his mom know Lexi had invited another partygoer.

His mom smiled at their approach. "You're getting very good, Lexi. Soon you'll be on TV, skating just like your brother."

Kentucky picked Lexi up and carried him to the table. "He's doing great. By the way, while we were on the ice, we ran into a friend. Lexi invited him to join us."

"No worries," she said, waving off Kentucky's words. "We have plenty of room for everyone. Who is this friend?" The way she asked left no room for doubt she was already assuming correctly.

"Rory," Lexi answered for him, proving he'd been listening to every word, as usual. "He likes trucks too."

Poor Rory. If he showed, Kentucky would learn

fast if he was really interested. Lexi could talk a man to death.

"Where do I put my gift?"

Kentucky caught his mom's expression before he had time to look behind him. Her face said it all. Rory was every bit as gorgeous as he thought. Everyone came to their feet. Rory held an envelope, looking nervous.

"I'll set it over here with the rest of his presents," his mom said, relieving Rory of the envelope.

"I don't have a card or anything, so I just wrote my name on the outside." He blew Kentucky away. Not only had he shown, he'd found a way to bring Lexi a present.

"You didn't have to do that," Kentucky said, feeling guilty.

Rory shrugged. "I'm not showing up to a birthday party empty handed. The woman at the front counter found the envelope for me. It was the best I could do on short notice." He tucked his hair behind his ear, looking shy. Kentucky wished he could set Rory at ease. He'd shown up. With a present for Lexi. Kentucky couldn't get past those two points.

He motioned toward his mom. "This is my mom, Lisa." They shook hands. Kentucky waved a hand toward his dad, who was still playing a nearby video game. "That's my dad, Brad. You probably saw him at the shop today. Of course, you've already met Lexi."

Rory nodded at everyone. "It's nice to meet you. I feel like I'm intruding on a family gathering, but I couldn't turn down Lexi's invitation. He asked so nicely."

"We're happy to have you," Lisa said, sounding every bit as welcoming as Kentucky knew she would. "As soon as Brad gets done being the biggest kid here, we'll have cake."

"Dad doesn't skate," Kentucky explained. He hoped with enough talking that Rory would stop looking like he'd gate crashed. He led Rory to the bench at the table. They sat. "Mom has always been the one to drag us onto the ice. She used to be a figure skater."

Lisa scoffed as she moved to reclaim her seat. "That was a long time ago, and I was mediocre at best."

Kentucky rolled his eyes at her false modesty. "She competed in the Olympics."

"Wow," Rory said, looking genuinely impressed. "That's amazing. Why aren't you skating tonight?"

She shrugged. A sad look passed over her

features. "I went down on the ice years ago and hit my head. I've had balance issues ever since. If I skate, someone has to hold my hand—like with Lexi. Since Brad doesn't skate, I just hang out on the sidelines."

"I'll go out with you," Rory offered. "Get some skates on. After cake and presents, you can hold my hand." He was genuine. Kentucky couldn't look away. No one had ever jumped in with both feet with his family before. This man who'd just met Kentucky had already shown up with a gift for Lexi and made his mom's night. Kentucky didn't know how to react. He kind of wanted to leave right then, stealing Rory away, and learning all there was to know about him.

Lisa chewed her bottom lip. It was beyond obvious she wanted to say yes. "Are you sure? That's a lot to ask in this rough Friday night crowd."

Rory didn't back down. In fact, he seemed just as thrilled as Lisa. "I'm positive. Get your skates. You should get to have fun too."

"Okay," Lisa said, sounding bright as she hopped to her feet. She focused on Kentucky. "I'll be right back. Don't let Lexi run off."

Kentucky nodded. "I've got him. Go." The moment she was gone, Kentucky switched his attention Rory's way. "That was really nice. She

13

doesn't get to do much anymore. You know, small child at home. Selfish husband," Kentucky said loud enough for his dad to hear.

"Eat me," Brad called over his shoulder, letting Kentucky know he was listening. "Your mom knows she's free to do as she pleases. As long as it pleases her to keep me happy," he tacked on.

Kentucky laughed. "He's joking. Sort of."

Rory's eyes flashed with good humor. "Your family seems nice."

"What about your family?"

Before Rory could answer Kentucky's question, Lexi shifted onto his knees and climbed into Rory's lap. He pulled a toy car from his pocket and showed it to Rory. "I have a car." Lexi made car noises as he pretended to drive the car across Rory's chest.

Rory held Lexi, ensuring he didn't tumble onto the floor. "That's amazing. It's fast." He cast Kentucky a quick glance. "My family wasn't nice," he said, keeping up with both conversations like a pro. "It's not important. I have a group of friends who are like my family now. We do everything together—like have Thanksgiving dinner and celebrate Christmas. But I don't have a normal family dynamic like this," he said, waving a finger at their surroundings.

"This family isn't normal," Brad said, joining them at the table. "Don't go into this thinking that or you'll run away screaming before the end of the night." He paused and eyed Rory. "You came in with that red Audi R8 today."

Rory nodded.

A line appeared between Brad's eyes. "You probably could've taken that to the dealership and gotten your oil changed for free. Don't they do that free for the first two years or something like that?"

Rory repositioned Lexi on his lap. "I bought the car when I lived in Los Angeles, and you have to take it to the original dealer to get the free oil change. Besides, how else could I stalk Kentucky properly if I didn't come to your shop?" He flashed Kentucky a smile and winked.

"I knew my son would come in handy somehow. What brought you here from Los Angeles?"

"I'm from here." Rory didn't appear to mind answering Brad's million questions while Lexi crawled all over him, using him a race track for his car. "When I graduated, my best friend Lucas and I decided to go to California and spend the summer. Kind of a senior trip of sorts. Anyhow, we made some friends there. They convinced us to stay four years longer than we intended, but the taxes there are outrageous. Finally, it drove us back home. I've been back almost a year now."

Kentucky did the math in his head. Rory had to be around twenty-two or three. He could work with that. Damn, he was young to have a car that cost close to two hundred thousand dollars. Kentucky had so many questions. Lisa reappeared with skates, talking a million miles a minute, showing her excitement. From that point, Kentucky lost Rory to his family. Rory fit right in, helping cut the cake and holding Lexi while he opened presents. All Kentucky could do was stare and enjoy the show.

TWO

RORY ADORED KENTUCKY'S FAMILY. HE HOPED the man knew how lucky he was. Lisa was incredibly sweet. She'd fed Rory more information in a couple hours than he could absorb. He'd learned she'd gotten sick after Kentucky was born and been told she couldn't have more kids. Fast forward twenty-three years later, when she was forty-two, lamenting the fact she'd probably never have grandkids, and surprise. She was pregnant with Lexi. He'd also learned Kentucky was a huge help and loved his brother more than life. Their family made Rory's chest hurt. He was happy for Kentucky and jealous for himself. Still, he was grateful for having met them. He hated to say goodbye.

As he waved to them in the parking lot,

Kentucky's hand slid across the small of his back. "My family loves you."

"They're amazing." Rory had a hard time concentrating on anything with Kentucky touching him.

"So are you. You realize fifty dollars is a lot of money to give a four-year-old."

Rory shrugged. "I have no idea what the going rate is on toys these days. It's not a big deal."

Kentucky's smile was amazing. Each time he smiled, Rory's gaze automatically slipped to the man's mouth. "It was a big deal to Lexi. He loved that. Would you like to grab a drink with me?"

"It was nice to make Lexi smile. I'm not much of a bar hopper," Rory admitted, hating that about himself in that moment. It was more about the people in bars than the bars themselves.

Kentucky's eyes flashed with wicked intent. "Actually, I thought we could have a drink at my place. That way, we can talk and actually hear each other." Kentucky's house sounded more dangerous than the bar. When he didn't respond right away, Kentucky shook his head. "Nope. Get that out of your mind. I promise you'll leave there un-accosted. I know you have no reason to believe me, but I've never had sex with anyone on a first date."

Oh no. Now Rory kind of wanted to be the first. No one should be so sexy they made someone want to be disrespected. "Okay." Damn. He was stupid.

Kentucky's smile made it worthwhile. "You can follow me there."

"I don't have my car," Rory admitted. "When I came to the party, I told my friends they could go on without me. I'd planned to call for a ride, but I can do that from your place later. If it's okay?"

"Or I could just take you home in the morning."

Even to Rory, his immediate smile felt blinding. "I thought you didn't have sex on the first date."

Kentucky draped a heavy arm across Rory's shoulders and steered him through the parking lot. "Oh, I didn't say anything about sex. I want a drink and I don't drink and drive. Plus, I kind of like the thought of keeping you all night. I want to know you."

An inner happy sigh rang through Rory's mind. He was like a kid on Christmas with Kentucky touching him. If the man knew how many times he'd fantasized about this moment, he'd run. "In the morning is fine. I'd like to know you too."

Kentucky led him to the passenger side of a black newer model F-250. Rory found his back against the door. Kentucky hovered over him, looking much larger than Rory anticipated. "Let's get something out of the way." Before Rory had time to question the statement, Kentucky's mouth covered his. Rory's body reacted like the man had dropped to his knees. His stomach muscles clenched in anticipation of the pleasure. Kentucky sank his teeth into Rory's bottom lip and tugged. A moan escaped Rory without a single fuck given. His palms found Kentucky's waist, feeling him up as he pulled him closer. Their tongues met. Rory fought the urge to climb Kentucky like a tree and rock his world. His whole body was on fire.

Kentucky cupped his face and went deeper, weakening Rory's knees. He didn't want to stop, but Kentucky pulled away. With his eyes closed and visibly fighting for breath, Kentucky was the sexiest man Rory had ever seen. Kentucky opened his eyes. He looked every bit as turned on as Rory. "Goddamn."

Yeah. Rory felt the same.

"Maybe I should take you home. I'm not sure I'll keep my hands to myself, after all."

"I don't want to go home." Rory's confession came out in a whisper. His throat didn't want to work.

Kentucky gave him a short nod and opened the door for Rory. "I'll try to behave."

"I can't make the same promise," Rory said as Kentucky closed the door. He wasn't sure if Kentucky heard him. Either way, Rory had tried to warn him. He was determined to have Kentucky. Maybe it wouldn't be tonight, but it would happen.

KENTUCKY HAD THOUGHT to kiss Rory and take the pressure off, hoping he wouldn't spend the whole night thinking about kissing him. Now, he couldn't think of anything else. As he watched Rory trail through his home, inspecting all his books and photos, his mind was trapped in a cycle. All he wanted was to lure Rory to the bedroom.

"Awwww. Lexi is short for Lexington. That's cute," Rory said, pointing to Lexi's birth announcement. "Do your parents have some odd Kentucky fetish?"

The question stole a chuckle from Kentucky. "They say Lexington, Kentucky is their fertile breeding ground. Once you really get to know my parents, you'll figure out they're a bit strange. My dad does these auto part conventions. It's a great way to travel and write it off on taxes. Anyhow, there's this huge convention every year in Lexington. My mom has only gone with him twice. Both times, she's gotten pregnant."

"That's sweet," Rory said as he moved to sit on the couch. "What about you? Do you travel a lot?"

Kentucky joined him, sitting as close as possible without an ounce of shame. "I used to. Back when I played hockey for Houston and New York, I traveled all the time. Of course, all I ever saw of every city was the airport, the arena, and the hotel. Still, I miss the travel. I'd like to see more places."

Rory leaned forward and tugged off his fleece. Kentucky didn't know how he'd stood it this long in the heat. Still, Kentucky enjoyed the show. Rory had a sleek body. It was made for sex. Kentucky had to take a breath through his nose, hoping to control his body. A tattoo of a wolf in pride colors covered Rory's forearm. It was bright and gorgeous. Kentucky found himself dragging his fingers along the design. "That's beautiful."

"Thank you." There was heat in Rory's tone. Kentucky's gaze snapped to his. That same heat was in Rory's eyes.

"You're beautiful."

Rory's gaze dropped to Kentucky's mouth before

returning to meet his stare. "You're making it hard to behave. I'd hate to ruin your streak of good behavior."

"Maybe I should grab those drinks for us."

Rory's eyebrows rose as if waiting to see which road Kentucky would choose. He stood before he fell on Rory with his dick out. Rory stood too and trailed behind him on the way to the kitchen, inspecting everything as they passed. "This is a nice place. Did you say you played hockey for Houston and New York?"

Kentucky nodded as he grabbed two beers from the fridge. "I was with Houston for seven years before moving to New York for one season. Unfortunately, I only played five games before getting hurt. Now, well, you see where I am now." He passed one beer Rory's way.

"The world needs mechanics more than it needs hockey players," Rory said, looking sincere.

"I suppose. What do you do?"

A knowing smile touched Rory's lips. "It's okay if you'd rather be playing hockey. Can you not go back to it?"

"It's unlikely another major team would touch me. I'm not sure if I want to go back to the minors." Kentucky shrugged and took a drink before explaining. "I spent seven years fighting to get picked up. If I went back, it would have to be for the love of the game, and nothing else. I wouldn't be working toward anything. The idea doesn't hold much appeal, but you never know."

Rory set his beer aside without taking a drink. With his back against the counter, he snagged Kentucky's shirt and hauled him closer. Kentucky watched it happen through hooded eyes. Damn, Rory made it hard to resist touching him.

"I think you should do what makes you happy," Rory said, towing Kentucky forward until he could wrap his arms around his neck. He had sincere eyes. Kentucky couldn't look away. "Would you be happier stuck in the minors or at your dad's shop? Don't think. Just answer."

"I don't know," Kentucky answered honestly.

A bright smile lit Rory's face. "You're not making it easy to help."

"Maybe I'm still figuring it out."

"I think maybe you should kiss me again."

At Rory's claim, Kentucky shuffled closer until their bodies touched. "Is that so?"

Instead of answering, Rory held his stare, obviously waiting for Kentucky to make a move.

"I'm trying to behave," Kentucky reminded him.

"It's almost midnight," Rory said, luring

Kentucky into being bad. "You've had a beer already. I think—technically—that makes this our second date."

Kentucky lowered his head. His eyes gave away his lust. "You're right. I don't hold any second date records."

RORY SNAPPED under the pressure of being in Kentucky's arms. Going up on his toes, he captured Kentucky's lips. Their tongues stroked, battling to get closer. Kentucky's hands were everywhere. Rory felt pulled in a dozen directions. He didn't know which move to make. With no real plan in mind, he urged Kentucky's shirt higher until Kentucky leaned away long enough to let him have it. With Kentucky's torso bare, Rory couldn't stop touching him. He was hard. Everywhere. Just large, solid muscle for Rory's hands to enjoy.

Beneath Kentucky's fingers, Rory's pants loosened. Kentucky's large hands found the bare globes of Rory's ass. He kneaded while urging Rory's body against his. Rory went for the button of Kentucky's jeans. His hands were forced away when

Kentucky pulled Rory's shirt up and dragged it over his head.

Kentucky eyed Rory's body for a moment. "Goddamn," he growled before reclaiming Rory's mouth. The feeling was mutual. Rory's dick leaked in his underwear, begging.

Rory's fingers found the button of Kentucky's jeans again. He managed to get it undone before—once again—his hands were forced away. This time, Kentucky spun him in his arms. Rory found himself clinging to the edge of the counter as Kentucky's teeth sank into his back. He gasped for air as Kentucky trailed tiny bites down his spine. Kentucky dragged Rory's jeans and underwear down as he went. He bit Rory's ass. A deep moan escaped Rory. He'd never been this close to coming with zero contact with his dick. Then, Kentucky reached around and boldly stroked Rory's cock. Rory dropped his forehead onto his hands at the edge of the counter. The pleasure weakened his knees. He couldn't stop the sounds falling from his lips. Kentucky fingered his asshole. A frisson ran through him.

"Please?" He gave no fucks over begging. Rory had never been hornier in his life. He heard the condom wrapper before he saw it hit the floor. His brain was stuck in hyperdrive. He needed release. Rory sucked in a breath as Kentucky probed at his ass, stretching him. Everything moved so fast. Nothing felt real.

"No," Kentucky said, pulling away and confusing Rory. "Not like this."

The world tilted, and a laugh caught in Rory's throat as he found himself slung over Kentucky's shoulder. He headed back toward the living room. Rory barely caught glimpses of the black kitchen appliances and dark marble countertops before they were on hardwood and headed for the dark leather couch.

Rory slid down Kentucky's body. The man's strength had Rory breathless. Kentucky sat, urging Rory to straddle his hips. Their lips met. This time, when Kentucky's cock pushed at Rory's asshole, it didn't feel as frantic.

"I think we're going to need more lube than what's on the condom."

A chuckle escaped Rory as he dropped his head to Kentucky's chest. His erection stared up at him, needing relief. "This isn't going well." Even he wasn't sure if he spoke to Kentucky or his dick.

Kentucky urged his chin up, forcing Rory to meet his stare. "This is going beautifully," he said, tightening Rory's throat with his sincerity. "It's just that you're really tight and I'm kind of big. I'm thinking this needs to move to the bedroom."

Damn. He was so sexy and sweet. They should've waited. One day, they'd probably both look back on this day and regret every minute.

RORY LOOKED WORRIED he was failing Kentucky in some way. Kentucky couldn't have the man feeling that way. In fact, the problem was the opposite. Rory was too perfect. Kentucky didn't think he'd last long enough to please Rory.

Determined to move slower, Kentucky gathered Rory against his chest and headed for the bedroom. He was a grown man. He could slow down. With Rory on the bed and some semblance of self-control returning, Kentucky found the lube. He crawled into bed beside Rory. Rory watched him with so much heat Kentucky couldn't resist recapturing his lips. Their kiss turned molten the second their lips met. Rory writhed beneath him—like he needed Kentucky or he'd die.

The moans and whimpers coming from Rory had Kentucky lubing the man's asshole, desperate to get inside him. Rory's short fingernails bit into Kentucky's shoulders when Kentucky fingered him. Kentucky fought for air. His dick twitched and leaked, ready to blow with no one touching it. Kentucky rolled, urging Rory to straddle his body. The moment he had Rory in position, Kentucky probed at the man's ass again, stretching, and pushing his way inside. Kentucky bit his bottom lip, trying to hold back a whimper. Rory was tight and perfect. He was hot and killing Kentucky.

Rory made a sound that had an involuntary twitch running through Kentucky. He was barely hanging on. Then, Rory spoke, making things worse. "You're so damn sexy. You've got me ready to come already." Rory sucked in an audible breath. "I can't remember the last time I wanted anyone this badly."

Kentucky couldn't get enough of Rory. He was vocal, expressive, and sexy as hell. The man left no room for doubt that Kentucky was doing the job he needed. It was the biggest turn-on he'd ever experienced. When he thought the moment couldn't get any hotter, Rory set his hand on Kentucky's jaw and held him in place, ensuring he couldn't look away as Rory rode his cock. Their gazes never wavered. The flush on Rory's cheeks deepened. He reached between them and stroked himself.

Kentucky couldn't have looked away if he tried. Rory's body tensed. A gasp escaped Kentucky. Pressure beat at his crown. His entire body tightened in anticipation. Rory's body began to spasm. In a move Kentucky had never experienced, Rory quickly covered Kentucky's eyes, protecting them from the jets of cum as they hit him. The move sent Kentucky over the edge. He'd never been with someone so sexual. As Rory leaned in and kissed him, Kentucky had a bad feeling he'd just been ruined for anyone else.

THREE

A GENTLE NUDGING DRAGGED RORY FROM THE deepest sleep he'd had in years. His eyes opened to the greatest sight—Kentucky hovering over him. A smile tugged at his lips before the memory of their night together filled his head, then it got brighter.

"Good morning, gorgeous." Damn. Even Kentucky's voice was hot. "You have no idea how much I hate waking you."

Kentucky was fully dressed. It was barely sunrise. The sight confused Rory. Disappointment settled in. Obviously, Kentucky was ready to get Rory out of his bed. "That's fine. I'll get dressed." He tried to sit. Kentucky stopped him.

He stroked Rory's hair. "I have a question."

"Okay." Rory wasn't sure what to think. Kentucky was being very loving for someone who was ready to be rid of him.

"I stayed up all night, thinking about your question. Around five, I made some calls and cashed in some favors. Skate-on tryouts for the Southeast minors are happening in New Orleans today. An agent friend of mine plans to meet me there to wheel and deal for me if I go. How do you feel about making the trip with me today to watch me try for a spot on a team this season? It's about a five-hour drive."

Kentucky didn't want him to leave. He wanted Rory to go with him. Rory sat up. He wasn't missing his chance to spend more time with Kentucky. "I'd love to. When do we need to leave?"

"Within an hour, if you can manage it?"

Rory stared down at himself. "I guess, if you don't mind me borrowing your shower or if I'm in yesterday's clothes, then sure."

Kentucky looked too excited to resist. "Make yourself at home. There're extra toothbrushes in my bathroom because my mom is a nurturer and a bulk buyer. If you want to borrow some clothes, feel free to dig through the closet and see if anything fits."

Rory's excitement grew. He had a hard time sitting still. Without thought, he bounced a little. "You're going to tryouts. I'm so thrilled for you. I'll hurry." He threw the covers back. Before he made it from the bed, he found himself trapped beneath Kentucky's six-foot-four frame. A whimper escaped him as Kentucky's teeth sank into the side of his neck. A groan vibrated against Rory's skin. "Sorry. You're nude and beautiful and I want to touch all your naughty bits."

Rory laughed, but only to hide his instant longing. Kentucky didn't move. Rory didn't either. He caressed Kentucky before holding him closer. Unexpectedly, his throat swelled. He didn't think he would get to keep Kentucky. People like Rory didn't find love. Not really. But Kentucky was in his arms right now. Rory inched Kentucky's shirt higher. "You'd be amazed how quickly I can get you off."

Another loud groan came from deep in Kentucky's chest. He rolled to the side, looking pained. "As much as I want to see you take up that challenge, we have to hurry if I want to get there on time."

Rory slipped from the bed. Kentucky couldn't be late. Kentucky wolf-whistled as Rory headed for the bathroom. Rory glanced over his shoulder, giving Kentucky his most seductive look. Kentucky linked his fingers behind his head, openly enjoying the show. Rory ensured he got all he could handle before closing the bathroom door. Kentucky's bathroom was huge. There were two walk-in closets with a Jacuzzi tub separating them. A large separate shower took up one wall while a gigantic vanity with a mirror above it took up the other. It had the lighting of Rory's dreams. Once Rory was out of sight, he went into overdrive. He shamelessly dug through Kentucky's stuff, finding the extra toothbrushes and rushing through his shower. Rory ran Kentucky's product through his hair and tried his best to not look like a homeless person before searching Kentucky's clothes for something close to his size. Kentucky was too tall and muscular. Rory made the best of things. His comfort didn't matter. He was ready in record time.

Rory found Kentucky loading his gear into the truck. He stood inside the open back door, watching the show. The way Kentucky's clothes stretched across his hard body fascinated Rory. He would've thought having seen what was beneath them would've lessened the impact Kentucky had on him. If anything, Rory's fascination had deepened. Kentucky turned and caught sight of Rory watching him. His face lit—like he'd spotted someone who made him happy.

"I see you found something to wear." Kentucky closed the distance between them and fingered the neck of the shirt. It was slipping down Rory's shoulder. "Damn, I think it's probably impossible for you to not look sexy."

Rory shrugged. The move had the shirt sliding farther down his shoulder. "I'm a survivor. You'd be surprised what I can make work under the right circumstances."

Kentucky dropped his mouth to Rory's bare shoulder and brushed a kiss across Rory's skin. "Gorgeous," he whispered, causing chill bumps to skirt through Rory. "Are you ready to get out of here? I'll grab us something to eat on the way."

"I'll buy," Rory offered, heading for the truck. He glanced over his shoulder and caught Kentucky staring at his ass. He bit back a knowing grin. Kentucky wasn't through with him yet. If Rory had his way, Kentucky never would be.

All the way to New Orleans, Rory pried as many stories as possible from Kentucky. He wanted to know every detail of the man's life. By the time they reached the arena, Rory had learned more than he'd ever dreamed. Kentucky was open about every aspect of his life. It was refreshing for someone like Rory. Someone who spent their time surrounded by fake smiles and fake everything.

Once inside the arena, Kentucky surprised him even more by proudly holding his hand as they made their way through the crowd. Rory did his best to keep up with Kentucky's long stride. He was easily the most confident person Rory had ever met. That was sexy. Kentucky motioned toward a man with platinum blond hair wearing a suit more expensive than most people's cars. The sight pulled Rory's thoughts away from the hundred and one things he liked about Kentucky. "There's my agent, Kieran."

Rory couldn't look away. The man was smooth, terrifying, and beautiful. His eyes were like gray ice. The only thing that kept Rory's feet moving in his direction was the toddler chewing on the man's tie. It cut the severity of his good looks. A second man appeared at his side and reached for the child, gently untangling the tie. When Mr. Too Severe looked at the dark-haired new arrival, everything changed. He turned human.

"Who's that with him?"

"Kieran's husband, Henley."

Rory nodded. "They're a nice-looking couple." It

was all Rory could think to say. They really were a gorgeous pair despite Kieran's hard demeanor.

Henley smiled at their approach. As if taking his human cues from his husband, Kieran did too. The pair met them halfway.

Kentucky smiled as he held a hand out to Kieran. "Hey, man. I feel like it's been forever."

Henley shook hands with Kentucky too. "You look ready to get back on the ice."

"I am. I've been staying in shape just in case." Kentucky motioned Rory's way. "This is Rory Vega." He waved toward Henley and Kieran. "This is Kieran and Henley Steele."

"It's nice to meet you," they each said simultaneously.

Rory couldn't help but laugh. They sounded like a choir.

Kentucky beamed. The sight made Rory's heart beat a little faster. Kentucky spoke, forcing Rory to pay attention to something other than his good looks. "Is it okay if Rory hangs out with you while I'm on the ice?"

"Of course," Kieran said brightly. "But you'd better get geared up. There're a ton of scouts, coaches, and owners here. They'll be starting soon."

Kentucky dipped his chin and pressed a quick

kiss to Rory's lips. "I'll be back before you have time to miss me."

"I'll be here." Rory watched him head into the locker rooms until he couldn't see Kentucky any longer before focusing on the pair who'd been left with him. "Who is this?" Rory asked, motioning toward the girl with tiny pigtails in Henley's arms. She looked somewhere between one and two years old.

Henley turned the little girl where she faced Rory. She had dark eyes, adorable cheeks, and looked to be of some sort of Asian descent. "This is our daughter, Mia. We're just adjusting to each other. She's only been with us two weeks, so we didn't want to leave her with a sitter."

Rory smiled and waved at her. She smiled back. "She's quiet."

Henley nodded. "I'm sure that'll change soon. She's nervous in this crowd."

Mia threw herself forward, leaving Rory no choice but to catch her. Still, he looked to Henley for permission before completely pulling Mia into his arms.

Henley nodded.

Rory settled the girl on his hip. "You are a doll," he told her while toying with her tiny fingers. "She weighs as much as one too. Wow, she's a tiny thing."

"She's lived in an orphanage her whole life," Kieran explained. "Since she's not a fighter and doesn't complain, she never got as much to eat as she should."

"Awww, that's heartbreaking," Rory said, incapable of tearing his eyes away from the little girl. They had so much in common. He wondered if she was old enough to understand how lucky she was. She'd been saved. Not everyone got that break.

"What is it about you?" Kentucky asked, reappearing from the locker room in full gear. "All kids love you."

Rory bit back a happy sigh at the sight of Kentucky in uniform. Damn. He'd had all of Kentucky and planned to enjoy it again. He tried concentrating on Kentucky's claim. "I like kids and I guess they know it."

"She's adorable," Kentucky said, brushing his finger down the girl's arm. She scrunched up her tiny body like it tickled. Kentucky focused on Kieran. "Thanks again for this. Guess I'd better get out there." He took a deep breath, showing his nerves.

"You'll be great." Rory used his brightest voice, hoping to lend him some confidence.

Kentucky winked. "Kiss for luck?"

Rory snagged his shirt and towed him in for a quick kiss. Mia giggled. Rory gasped. "She does make sound."

Kentucky skated onto the ice, leaving Rory alone with his friends again. Rory watched him go while holding his breath. He wanted Kentucky to be amazing so he could have his dream back. He focused on Kieran and Henley once more. They had their heads together, talking quietly. When they noticed him watching, they straightened, and flashed him matching smiles.

"So, um," Henley said, looking nervous. "We were wondering, can we have your autograph?"

Oh, shit. "Sure," Rory said brightly, silently thanking every deity they'd waited until after Kentucky left.

"Are you positive? We don't want to make you uncomfortable." Henley looked so genuine. He didn't realize it was impossible to make Rory uncomfortable.

"It's no problem at all," Rory said, waving off the man's concerns. "Let's grab a seat and I'll sign whatever you like." Then he'd do his best to turn the conversation to something different. His career was the absolute last thing he wanted to spend the day talking about.

———

ON THE DRIVE BACK HOME, Rory was quieter than he'd been on the drive to New Orleans. Kentucky was too, but he was tired. It stood to reason Rory was too, but Kentucky wanted to hear his voice. He glanced over, hoping to prod Rory into finding a topic. He was asleep. A smile tugged at Kentucky's lips. Between the five-hour drive to New Orleans, the four-hour assessment period, and now a five-hour drive home, Kentucky wasn't surprised Rory was out. He went back to staring at the road. Kentucky had dragged the poor guy all over the place in the past twenty-four hours. Even in borrowed clothes way too big for him, Rory still handled himself with grace while looking sexy as sin. Kentucky had left him with strangers. Not just any strangers either, but Kieran and Henley Steele. When he'd come off the ice, the trio had been talking and laughing like old friends. Rory never ceased to impress him. Anyone else would've run screaming under Kieran's cold demeanor. Not Rory. He was a chameleon, fitting in everywhere he went.

When he reached Houston, as much as Kentucky didn't want to, he woke Rory. "Hey, sexy. I need your address so I can get you home."

Rory sat up straight, blinking. "Um, sorry. I didn't mean to fall asleep." He looked around. "Damn, I missed the whole drive. I'm boring company."

The smile pulling at the corners of Kentucky's mouth was out of his control. Rory was adorable. "I didn't ask you to come along to entertain me. I just wanted more time with you."

"Thank you for letting me tag along. I had fun watching you show off your skills. Turn right up here," he said, motioning toward the next street.

Kentucky did as told. Now that he was on his way to take Rory home, he wasn't ready to give him up yet. He cleared his throat, hoping not to sound like an idiot. "Um, I know you're probably ready to get home to your bed and your clothes, but how do you feel about grabbing some clothes and staying another night with me?" Another thought hit him. "I'm not asking for sex, especially since my entire body hurts."

Rory brushed his fingers down his arm. "Oh no. Are you okay? What can I do to help?"

He sounded so worried, Kentucky found himself

rushing to reassure him. "I'm okay. It's just been a while since I've gone through the motions. I forgot how hard hockey is on the body."

Out of the corner of his eye, he saw Rory nod. "Don't worry. I'll take care of you. Turn left at the next stop sign and then right after two streets. My house is on the left. I'll point to it when we get there."

As Kentucky followed Rory's directions, the houses got larger and more extravagant. His discomfort rose. "You know, I don't think you ever answered me when I asked what you do for a living."

A light laugh filled the car. "I do freelance work for the entertainment industry, but it's a lot cheaper living here than it is in California. In Cali, I was paying twice as much for one-third the house, so—to me—it's a lot more economical than it seems. It's that one," Rory said, pointing to a house that looked completely out of Kentucky's league, and Kentucky wasn't poor. That one year in the majors had been nothing to sneeze at. As he pulled into the driveway, Rory took off his seatbelt. "Give me five and I'll grab a bag. When we get back to your place, I'll make you better."

At Rory's promise, Kentucky forgot all his questions. "I'll be waiting."

With a wink, Rory slipped from the truck and rushed to the door. Kentucky didn't look away until Rory closed the door behind him. Rory was back in less than five, impressing Kentucky. He was even more blown away when Rory didn't stop at his seat. Instead, he climbed across the console between them and captured Kentucky's lips. He tasted like mint, as if he'd brushed his teeth while inside. That was the last thought Kentucky had. His mind couldn't hold on to anything beneath Rory's skilled tongue. Before Kentucky had time to gather his wits, Rory was back in his seat, buckling his belt.

"Are you ready?" Rory sounded completely unaffected, but his cheeks were flushed. That was good enough for Kentucky.

By the time he climbed from the truck at home, Kentucky was biting his bottom lip to keep from groaning like an old man. Everything hurt. He was so stiff. Rory flashed him a knowing look before following him inside. Kentucky dropped his gear by the door. He didn't have the fortitude to carry it any farther. Rory took his hand and led him to the couch. His concerned gaze warmed Kentucky's heart.

"Sit here," Rory demanded, pointing toward the couch. "I'll be right back."

Kentucky sat. With his curiosity piqued, he

watched Rory disappear inside his bedroom with his bags. Several minutes passed. Kentucky almost went looking for him when Rory returned. He was shirtless and wearing only fleece shorts. Kentucky damn near swallowed his tongue.

He waved for Kentucky to join him. "Okay. Let's go."

Kentucky didn't question his luck. He jumped to his feet and followed. All his thoughts about sore muscles were gone. Rory waited. When Kentucky reached his side, Rory took his hand and led him to the bathroom. He motioned toward the tub. It was filled with steaming water and bubbles. "Tada. Get in."

He couldn't remember the last time he'd taken an actual bath. Rory had gone through the trouble, so he stripped. The water was the perfect temperature. An unexpected sigh escaped as he settled in. Rory urged Kentucky's head back against the rim, slipping a rolled-up towel beneath his neck for comfort. "Close your eyes. I won't let you drown."

Kentucky closed his eyes. Rory touched his chest. It took him a second to realize Rory had massaged something into his skin. The sweet smell overcame him. Kentucky couldn't concentrate on anything other than the way Rory's hands felt on his skin. He massaged Kentucky's arms, shoulders, and chest before moving lower. Five seconds in, Kentucky had gone hard. Now, with Rory's touch heading south, Kentucky's lips parted on a pant. He'd long past forgotten feeling old. Rory's fingers dug into his skin, working away all the kinks. Kentucky almost groaned when Rory bypassed where he wanted him the most. Instead, he moved to the end of the tub to Kentucky's feet. Rory left no spot on his legs and feet untouched. By the time he was close to Kentucky's erection again, Kentucky was barely resisting the urge to stroke himself. Without warning, Rory's fingers skimmed Kentucky's cock. A gasp escaped him. He was already on edge from the anticipation. Just as Rory had done during sex, his every move was mind blowing. While holding Kentucky's cock in place at the root with one hand, Rory pumped with the other. He didn't tease or lose rhythm. Rory kept the perfect pace and pressure to have Kentucky holding the sides of the tub and fighting the urge to openly fuck Rory's hands.

Kentucky didn't open his eyes. He let everything happen to him. Rory was too perfect. Kentucky didn't have the strength to do anything except enjoy what the man offered. Rory made him feel like he must've been very good in a previous life to deserve this.

Sounds escaped him and bounced off the walls of the bathroom. There was no slowing down. Rory made it impossible for Kentucky to catch his breath. His touch was merciless. Pressure beat at his crown. Ecstasy was just out of reach. Then, Rory's lips touched his. That was it. It was the tiniest pressure with slightly parted lips—like a sharing of oxygen. Kentucky came unglued. Pleasure slammed into Kentucky hard enough to stop his heart. He snagged the back of Rory's head and licked the man's tongue before he could get away. Rory fought every bit as hard as Kentucky to get closer. Even when Kentucky's sanity returned a hair, he didn't let up. Kentucky couldn't get enough of Rory. He was perfect.

"You need a shower now," Rory said with a chuckle against Kentucky's lips.

"Join me."

"Hmmm, let me think about it. Okay." Rory stood and moved to the shower. He got the water started as Kentucky pulled the plug in the bathtub. Kentucky turned his head at just the right time to watch Rory strip. Every inch of the man, including the erection standing proud and waiting for Kentucky's touch, was perfection.

"Wow."

Rory glanced over at the involuntary comment. "What?" It was like he didn't realize what he did to Kentucky's mind and heart.

Kentucky pushed from the tub. He held Rory's stare as he crossed the room. As their bodies collided, Kentucky walked Rory backward into the shower. He didn't stop until water streamed down their bodies and their lips met. It was a sweet kiss full of promise. Kentucky tried to keep it that way, but he couldn't ignore Rory's erection pressed between them. He palmed the man's cock as his lips moved to Rory's jaw. From there, he moved to the side of Rory's neck. He trailed light kisses until he found the spot where Rory's neck and shoulder met. Kentucky stopped there, letting his lips linger. He kept his touch light, making slow love to Rory with his hands. They felt real. Kentucky couldn't explain it. He just knew.

"Do you feel that?" he whispered against Rory's skin. "There's more than sex between us."

Rory's fingers dug into Kentucky's biceps. "Yes." He sounded breathless and sexy, but every bit as positive as Kentucky.

"Good. I don't want to stop." Kentucky hoped Rory understood. He wasn't finished touching him. He didn't want to stop being with him. This wasn't a weekend fling. Kentucky planned to make Rory fly, and then they'd go to bed. He would hold Rory while they slept, and when tomorrow came, they'd start all over again. Kentucky was happier than he'd ever been. He didn't want it to stop.

FOUR

Kentucky: *Is it just me or can you not stop thinking about last weekend too?*

Rory: *It's like you read my mind. I've been fighting the urge to text you this for two hours.*

Kentucky: *Never fight your urges with me. I want to hear from you.*

Rory: *I won't waffle next time. How's your day going?*

Kentucky: *It'll be better in three hours when I get off work. I'm hoping I can see you. If you're not sick of me, that is.*

Rory: *Three hours... I'll be waiting in your driveway.*

Kentucky: *It's too hot for that. There's a key*

under a rock in the flower bed by the front door. Wait inside.

Rory: *Okay. See you then.*

Kentucky: *Can't wait.*

RORY: *Tired of me yet?*

Kentucky: *I don't think that's possible. Why?*

Rory: *I'm in the mood for steak, but I don't want to cook. So I was hoping you'd let me take you to dinner.*

Kentucky: *You know what time I get off. I'd love to see you, steak or not.*

Rory: *I'll be waiting when you get home.*

Kentucky: *I can't wait.*

RORY: *Do I need to come up with an excuse to be waiting?*

Kentucky: *Absolutely not. This has been the longest day ever and I miss you like crazy. Knowing you'll be there when I get home is the only thing that keeps me sane some days.*

Rory: *How about this? Let's just assume I'll be waiting unless one of us says otherwise.*

Kentucky: *I like this plan. See you soon.*

Rory: *Hugs.*

KENTUCKY: *I just wanted to say these past few weeks with you have been the best of my life. Every time I have to tell you goodbye, those are the worst moments of my life.*

Rory: *It's like you stole all my words. I feel the same way.*

Kentucky: *Good, because you're not getting rid of me.*

Rory: *Awesome. All my nefarious plans are coming to fruition.*

Kentucky: *MWHAHA.*

LISA: *What are you doing today?*

Rory: *Nothing. What did you have in mind?*

Lisa: *A day of shopping. **hopeful face***

Rory: *I'd love to.*

Lisa: *Yay. Send me your address and I'll pick you up.*

RORY: *I might be a little late tonight. I talked your mom into getting a new hairstyle she's been too scared to try.*

Kentucky: *You have a habit of talking my mom into things. I'll be here when you're done.*

Rory: *Good, because I miss you.*

Kentucky: ***whimpers** same.*

KENTUCKY: *My dad says thanks for the new hairstyle. You made my mom happy.*

Rory: *I just sat with her. She was the brave one.*

Kentucky: *Still. You're amazing.*

Rory: *xoxo*

RORY: *My friends want to meet you. They're accusing me of keeping you hidden.*

Kentucky: *We can't have that. I don't want to be hidden.*

Rory: *You might change your mind once you meet them. We're having a pool party slash cookout at my house tomorrow. How does two o'clock sound?*

Kentucky: *I'll be there.*

Rory: *Bring something to swim in.*

Kentucky: *Anything else?*

Rory: *Nope. Just you. Try not to be too sexy. I don't want to fight everyone for your attention.*

Kentucky: *Swim trunks and my regular face. Got it.*

Rory: *Grrr. Don't make me spank you.*

Kentucky: *Promises. Promises.*

IN A MATTER OF MINUTES, Kentucky would be there. Rory didn't know whether to cheer or cry. His friends weren't for everyone. All Rory could do was pray they behaved. Being good wasn't often on Lucas, Bryson, Shawn, or Jay's agenda. Unless they were being good at it. That they could do. Unfortunately, he couldn't keep Kentucky to himself forever. He'd already gone too long without introducing him to his chosen family. As nervous as he was, the moment the doorbell sounded, Rory found himself rushing to the door. He was so stupid over Kentucky. It hadn't been that long since they'd last seen each other. Hours really. Still, he couldn't get to the man fast enough to suit his heart.

He paused for a half a heartbeat with his hand on the doorknob and took a deep breath. Once he was certain he didn't look like he'd just run for the door, he turned the knob. At the first sight of Kentucky's gorgeous blue eyes, Rory's heart skipped a beat. While wearing a red and white striped tank top and red shorts, Kentucky looked sexy as sin with his swimming trunks slung over his shoulder. Fuck, it was ridiculous. Rory thought every little thing the man did was perfect. He couldn't control his smile. Happiness sounded in his voice.

"Hey." Even to Rory, he sounded breathless.

Kentucky snagged Rory's shirt and towed him in for a kiss. "Hey," he whispered against Rory's lips.

Rory hopped backward, feeling like a little kid in his excitement. "Come in."

As Kentucky stepped over the threshold, a line appeared between his eyes. "You know, I've just realized this is the first time I've been inside your house. That seems odd."

It was true. The move hadn't really been

purposeful. They just always ended up staying at Kentucky's place. "I hadn't thought about it, but you're right."

Kentucky looked in every direction, taking in the place. "Um, can we revisit the topic of what you do for a living? This place is amazing."

Rory laughed. "I live here with four other people. Trust me, splitting the bills five ways makes it dirt cheap. My friend Jay is the actual owner though."

"Okay, but still, I've never seen you work, and this place... wow."

Rory took Kentucky's hand and headed for the back door. "Considering I work online and while you're at work, you wouldn't see it. Plus, it's not exactly steady work."

Kentucky dragged his feet, making it impossible for Rory to rush him outside to introduce him to everyone. "If it isn't steady, how do you pay your part of the bills?"

Rory shrugged. He kept his gaze locked straight ahead, hoping he didn't give away how evasive he was being. "My work is freelance, and I do some graphic design stuff. It comes and goes, so I've learned to save for rainy days. Plus, I get royalties from different projects I've worked on over the years.

Come meet my friends," he said, throwing open the back door and cutting off the conversation. His friends were huddled around the grill, arguing over the best way to cook each item. The way they always did. Bryson would win. He always did. Lucas and Jay would give up first because they were too into each other to bother with anything else for long. Shawn would argue the longest because he loved watching Bryson lose his temper. Then he'd give in gracefully, enraging Bryson further. Things never changed around their house.

"Hey, guys, come meet Kentucky," Rory called as he circled the pool to the other side of the portico.

They turned as a unit. As if they'd planned the move ahead of time, they each dropped their gazes to Kentucky's toes before slowly undressing him with their eyes. Kentucky shifted uncomfortably under their stares. Rory bit back a chuckle.

Shawn, the ginger of the bunch, stepped forward first. He lowered his shades, showing off his amazing green eyes. "Hey, gorgeous. Welcome to our humble abode. I hope you like overcooked and under seasoned food, because that's what Bryson will be serving at some point today," he said, motioning to an obviously irritated Bryson at his back. He held a hand out for Kentucky. "I'm Shawn, by the way."

Kentucky shook his hand. "Nice to meet you."

Bryson pushed him aside. "I'm Bryson. He's an idiot. I'm an amazing chef and he won't hesitate to eat all this off my ass later."

With a chuckle, Kentucky shook Bryson's hand too, before Lucas took over.

He passed Rory his drink before holding his hand out for Kentucky to shake. "Lucas," he said, sounding as calm as always. Lucas was the still waters in their group. He was also Rory's best friend, and the one Rory had known the longest.

Jay didn't have time to introduce himself before Kentucky focused on him. "You look familiar. Where have I seen you?"

Rory's insides froze.

Jay beamed. "I don't know. Have you ever been to L.A.? I haven't lived here long and would definitely remember meeting you."

Kentucky closed one eye as if that would help him remember. Despite the shaking in Rory's stomach, Kentucky looked adorable. He snapped his fingers. "You used to do commercials for that one makeup line, right?"

Somehow, Jay's smile brightened. He absently stroked Lucas' stomach. "Yaaaas, queen. I didn't even think of that. That was so long ago. I was a teenager. Practically still a baby."

Kentucky made a dismissive noise. "You're still practically a baby." Before Jay could blush and argue, Kentucky focused on Rory. "May I use your restroom? I also need to change," he added, pulling the trunks from his wide shoulders.

"Sure." Rory motioned toward a nearby set of French doors. "If you go through there, that's my bedroom. You can use the one in there."

With a wink, Kentucky headed that way. Rory watched his ass for every step.

"Wow. He really doesn't know who you are, does he?" Lucas said the second Kentucky was out of earshot.

Rory took a sip of Lucas' drink before handing it back. "Nope."

"Wow," Lucas repeated, sounding floored. "That has to be a first. It's also kind of sweet."

"You should tell him," Jay cut in, wiping away Rory's joy over finding a nice guy who knew nothing about Rory.

"You definitely should," Shawn said, throwing in his two cents. "This isn't the kind of thing you keep to yourself."

Jay, Lucas, and Bryson nodded along with Shawn. Bryson was the one who spoke up. "If you really like him, you have to be honest. He's a big guy. What if he loses his shit when he finds out? You could get hurt."

Jay looked upset. Rory wished everyone would shut up. It was obvious they were reminding Jay of the past. "You should stick to your crowd," Jay said, sounding panicked and confirming Rory's thoughts. "Nothing good can come of this."

The more they spoke, the more the pressure grew in Rory's chest. "Just let me handle this my way," Rory snapped. He took a breath and tempered his voice. "I really like this guy, y'all. Please let me deal with things in my own time. Plus, for all we know, he might just be pretending he doesn't know me. He doesn't know I recognized him right away. It could go both ways."

Shawn rubbed Rory's back. "It's okay. This is your thing. You're allowed to have a life too. Handle things your way."

Unfortunately, now that they'd all made valid points, Rory felt like shit for not being honest. He liked Kentucky. Possibly he more than liked him. In truth, he couldn't find the words to tell Kentucky everything. He wasn't ready to lose him. "I'll be back," he said, stepping around them, and heading for the house. They were right. He should say something. The longer he stayed silent, the worse things would be. He spotted Kentucky the moment he cleared the door. Kentucky was eyeing the photos on Rory's shelf.

He flashed Rory a smile over his shoulder. "You weren't kidding about your friends being your family. There isn't a single picture of your family."

Rory moved to the bed. After crawling onto the king-sized mattress, he sat cross-legged and stared at Kentucky. He looked so sexy in his swimming trunks. Rory wanted to lick him. Instead, he stayed on topic. He needed to tell Kentucky everything. "Not everyone is as lucky as you are."

"You're not unlucky. Your friends seem great," Kentucky said, closing the distance between them.

Rory watched his approach with his heart in his throat. He didn't know where to start. "I have something I need to tell you."

Kentucky crawled onto the bed. He kept moving until he forced Rory onto his back. His large body covered Rory. "Yeah, I have something I need to tell you too." Kentucky hovered over him. Rory had an odd thought. He really loved the way Kentucky's hips felt against his inner thighs. Kentucky swept Rory's hair away from his face. His gaze moved over

Rory's face. Rory held his breath. Kentucky didn't say anything.

"I thought you had something to tell me," Rory said quietly, scared to break the spell.

"You're beautiful. It stole my thoughts for a second." A happy inner sigh rose in Rory. Kentucky didn't stop there. "I miss you a lot when you're not around."

A lump swelled in Rory's throat.

Kentucky kept going, stealing more of Rory by the moment. "It's hard for me not to rush you and I don't even know what I'm rushing toward. I just don't want to be anywhere else other than where you are. You make me better."

Rory tugged on the band in Kentucky's hair, setting his locks free. His heart was full. It was hard not to pretend they were in a bubble where it was only them.

"What did you want to tell me?"

Rory didn't answer right away and the confession he'd intended wouldn't come. Instead, he ran his fingers through Kentucky's hair, creating a curtain around the man's face. "I was raised in a group home. That's why there're no pictures of my family. I literally have no family. All I've ever had is my friends."

Kentucky's gaze moved over Rory's face. He looked more serious than Rory could remember seeing him. "You have me."

While holding Kentucky's stare, Rory cupped Kentucky's face, drawing him closer and joining him inside the curtain of hair. "I could see myself in love with you," Rory said as he touched his lips to Kentucky's. Maybe he was there already. He didn't know. Rory had never been in love. Not even close. But Kentucky felt right—like there was no one else he wanted to be with again. He wanted to hear every detail about Kentucky's day. Rory just wanted to sit at his side and hold his hand. Kentucky was warm and safe. He was the loving hand Rory had never felt caressing his life. His soul. The thought of losing him terrified Rory. He couldn't let it happen.

I COULD SEE myself in love with you. Those words rang in Kentucky's ears. Kentucky could more than see himself in love with Rory. He was ninety-five percent certain he was already there. The other five percent was the part of him that was scared Rory was too good to be true. No one else motivated him or cared more about his happiness more than their own. Rory did. It was addictive. Plus, the man's kiss... damn. He moved Kentucky.

The way their lips clung and tongues brushed; it was magical. He'd come to meet Rory's friends, but it was like the world had disappeared. They were alone. Nothing else mattered. His fingers found the only two buttons that were buttoned at the center of Rory's Panama shirt. He popped them loose. His mouth followed the trail of his fingers. The need to taste every inch of Rory was real and crippling. Rory's skin was still warm from obviously being in the sun all day. He smelled like coconut. Kentucky's mouth opened over Rory's nipple. He scraped his teeth over the bud. Rory held his head and moaned. The sound vibrated against Kentucky's lips, driving him wild. He moved lower, dragging open-mouthed kisses down Rory's body. Kentucky knew he should stop. They needed to rejoin the party. He couldn't pull away. Those fucking words. *I could see myself in love with you.* Kentucky's fingers curled around the edge of Rory's speedo. The material slipped down Rory's hips like all it had been waiting for was the slightest urging from Kentucky. His tongue found the slight indention running down the center of Rory's stomach. He traced it until Rory's crown was between his lips. Rory's hips left the bed. A whimper filled the air. Kentucky swore he had no plan to go this far. There was no stopping it now. Rory's pre-cum tasted too damn good. Kentucky kept licking and sucking, searching for more. He needed the salt. The moans. Rory belonged to him.

Kentucky was merciless. He treated Rory like a meal. The sounds coming from Rory said he enjoyed the attention, but it wasn't even about that anymore. Kentucky was half mad with the need to taste Rory's cum. He couldn't stop sucking, trying to get more in his mouth. Rory scratched at his skin and moaned. Kentucky held his hips in place, forcing him to endure the torment. Rory pulled his hair, holding on as he fucked Kentucky's mouth with zero shame.

"Goddamn. Yes. Suck me. Fuck. That feels good. Take it all."

At Rory's demand, Kentucky took him down his throat before releasing him, only to suck him harder. A gasp bounced off the walls. Rory's body went stiff. Cum flooded Kentucky's mouth faster than he could swallow. Rory's body shook as Kentucky licked away the mess.

"Jesus. Holy shit."

Kentucky crawled up Rory's body and captured his lips. His heart demanded more. He'd never felt so desperate to own someone in every way. It wasn't about sex. This was something primal. The way he felt about Rory was so powerful, it didn't want to be contained. "Run away with me," Kentucky begged, pulling a chuckle from Rory.

Rory stroked his face. "We're adults. We don't have to run away to be together."

Kentucky chased Rory's thumb so he could place a kiss on its pad. "I don't care. Let's run away anyhow. We can live in the woods like wild men. Ditch our clothes and pick berries to survive."

Rory's entire body shook beneath him with laughter. "Okay. We could do that, or I could pack a bag and we could go to your place. Let's sneak away. We could turn off our phones, close the blinds, and pretend we're alone in the world."

Kentucky wanted the picture Rory painted. Fuck the rest of the world. "What about your friends?"

Rory shrugged. "They'll survive without us. I guarantee Jay and Lucas have already slipped away and Shawn is doing his damnedest to seduce Bryson while they're alone. They won't even miss us."

Kentucky scrambled to his feet. His hard dick cried over the thought of not getting immediate relief. He didn't care. Kentucky pulled Rory to his feet. "I'll help you pack. Tell me where to start."

Rory's smile let him know he'd made the right choice. He wasn't the only one who wanted this for real. "Get my bag from the closet. I'll get my toiletries together."

With a nod, they headed in different directions with the same goal in mind. They were stealing a life together, hoping for a future where they were never apart.

FIVE

It had been the best week of Kentucky's life. When he'd asked Rory to run away with him, he'd gotten everything he'd wanted. The first weekend had been amazing. Kentucky felt certain he'd made love to Rory in every room and in every possible way. He'd turned into a glutton with Rory beneath his roof. When Monday arrived, and Kentucky had to work, he hadn't been able to stop himself from begging Rory not to leave. Rory being Rory, he'd cupped Kentucky's face, kissed him, and promised to stay as long as Kentucky liked. Even with that vow in place, Kentucky had rushed home each day, scared to death Rory wouldn't be there. Rory hadn't let him down. Every night, he was there.

Kentucky brushed his hand down Rory's thigh.

It was Saturday night, and it seemed as if he should take the man somewhere. But after Rory cooked him the spaghetti he'd promised Kentucky had been missing by eating the sauce in a jar, he'd curled up next to Kentucky on the couch and passed out. Several times, he'd thought to wake him. Instead, Kentucky sat in silence and stared. Sooner or later, Rory would have to go home. Kentucky couldn't expect the man to put his life on hold forever. But maybe... Kentucky's phone rang, cutting off his line of thinking before it went too deep. He dug his phone out while trying not to wake Rory. When he spotted Kieran's name, he slipped from the couch and rushed to the bedroom out of earshot. It had been eight weeks since skate-on tryouts and he hadn't heard a thing. Even though he hadn't completely given up hope, since he knew with his past it wouldn't be a quick thing, doubts had been creeping in.

"Hello?"

"Hey, it's Kieran. How are you?"

Kentucky tried to stamp down his growing excitement. "I'm good. How are you?"

"I'm great. Listen, I've been in talks with the owner of the Ice Flames in Jackson, Mississippi this week. He wants you to sign." Kentucky barely stopped himself from shouting in his elation. Kieran kept talking, killing his joy. "The thing is, George Lowe is an ultra-conservative. He's not crazy about taking on an openly gay player, but he's all about loving the sinner. Along with a bunch of other bullshit I had to sit through and won't repeat. But he drew a hard line at taking on an openly gay player who's also dating a porn star. If you want to sign with him, you can't keep seeing Rory." Kentucky almost laughed aloud at the insinuation, but Kieran didn't stop there. "I told him I'd talk to you because I wasn't sure if your relationship was serious. You have two weeks to make up your mind. If you want my two cents, I think you should pass. There're other teams and other team owners who'll stay out of your private business. Once this guy signs you, he could become a real pain. Hell, you could find yourself trying to climb in the closet to keep him happy. I don't know if anything is worth that. Plus, Henley and I like Rory. This is a shitty position to be in."

Once Kentucky was sure Kieran was finished, he had to clear his throat to respond. His mind raced. Nothing wanted to work properly, especially his tongue. Kieran's claim kept banging on his brain, doing as much damage as possible. "Um, okay. Yeah. I definitely need to think about it. Everything you've said sounds horrible." That was the understatement of the year. Kentucky prayed the part about Rory wasn't true. In fact, he had no idea where that bullshit came from.

Kieran made a sympathetic noise. "I figured you would. Like I said, you have two weeks. Take them. Decide what you want. In the meantime, I'll keep looking at other options."

Kentucky nodded, even though Kieran couldn't see him. "Okay. Thank you. I can't tell you how much I appreciate your help."

"It's what I do. I'll talk to you soon."

"Yeah. Talk to you later," Kentucky pushed out past his tight throat. The moment the call disconnected, Kentucky stared at the face of his phone. It wasn't true. It couldn't be. Then again, he hadn't really thought about how smoothly Rory always dodged his questions about work.

While twirling the phone between his hands, Kentucky headed back to the living room. He sat and stared at Rory. His dark hair had fallen in his face. Kentucky brushed it aside. He was so beautiful. Breathtaking, really. Kentucky could see it. He could imagine men tripping over themselves to pay to watch Rory in action. Hell, he had firsthand experience with Rory's skills. It was some expert-level shit. He'd impressed Kentucky in every way possible.

"Is everything okay?" Rory mumbled, sounding more asleep than awake.

Kentucky swallowed past the pain. "Kieran just called."

Rory sat up. He looked sleep-swollen and sweet, but he was obviously invested in what happened with Kentucky's career. Kentucky wanted to take him to bed. Hold him. Pretend the last ten minutes never happened. "What did he say? Is there an interested team?" He looked hopeful and excited. Rory cared. His reactions were genuine. It was like a knife to the chest.

"Yeah. A team from Jackson, Mississippi wants me."

Rory cheered. "That's awesome." He shifted to his knees, getting into the conversation. "Tell me everything."

Kentucky rubbed his chest. "They want me on one condition. It seems the team's owner is a religious zealot."

Rory's smile fell. "Oh no."

"He said if I sign with him, I can't keep dating you."

The reaction was swift. Rory's expression

snapped closed. He didn't respond.

Kentucky couldn't take it. "Is it true?" He didn't expound. If it was true, he didn't think there could be any misunderstanding about what he meant.

Rory visibly swallowed. A pained look crossed his features. "Probably."

Words abandoned Kentucky. He toyed with the phone between his hands. He dropped his gaze to his lap. Kentucky couldn't stop clearing his throat. It was like his heart was stuck there. "I'm guessing Jay and all them are..."

"Yes."

Kentucky's eyes fell closed. His brain had given out. He knew there should be things to say. A sane man should scream, throw shit, react in some way, but Kentucky had nothing. Since meeting Rory, his life had been getting better every day. His future had never looked so bright. Now he couldn't see past the pain. He had questions. They wouldn't form. It was like he was broken.

KENTUCKY WAS SCARING the hell out of Rory. His silence was deafening. Rory knew they needed to talk, but he wondered if he shouldn't leave instead. Kentucky watched his lap, refusing to look at Rory. The pain rolling off Kentucky in waves was choking Rory. He couldn't move.

Someone needed to be the one to start. Rory knew it should be him. After all, he'd been silent too long already and hurt the person he cared about the most. Rory picked a place and started talking. "Lucas and I went to California at eighteen. We just found our crowd and started partying. One night, we were very high, and Shawn was like, 'Hey, you guys know you can make a lot of money for stuff you're already doing. Then you could stay here and party with us all the time.'" Rory twisted his fingers, feeling exposed. "So we jumped in. It was pretty amateur stuff. That didn't seem to matter. We picked up a following pretty quick. Then we were introduced to Jay and Bryson. They were pros who already had a huge contract. We did one film and things exploded." Rory fought a nervous laugh at the unintended pun. He took a deep breath. "Jay moved us in and we became a web sensation. We had people paying monthly fees to watch the five of us together. The money was more than I expected to ever make, since I never expected to go anywhere in life. Something really horrible happened to Jay. It shook all of us pretty hard, so we decided to move back home. Shawn, Jay, and Bryson came with us. Then, I met you."

"You let me hang out with people you fuck all day and didn't say a word." Kentucky's voice was dead. "I introduced you to my family. We made love several times, and you didn't think any of that was need-to-know information?"

It was like someone was sitting on his chest. He couldn't breathe. Kentucky sounded like every man he'd ever met, but this time, it mattered. "I like you." Rory made a helpless gesture that came from his soul. His brow pulled together in a frown as he swallowed down the bitterness. "I like you," he repeated, unsure of how to get his point across. His words didn't feel adequate. "If I'd told you the day we met, would you have bothered getting to know me? Or would you have thought it was cool to fuck me and move on? I wanted you to know me for me. To like me for me. Not think I'm some whore who fucks for money."

Kentucky's chin finally lifted. Their gazes met. "Do I strike you as the type to treat anyone that way?"

"I didn't know you," Rory said, trying his heart out to explain. "I was scared."

Kentucky shook his head. His hands lifted before

falling back to his lap. "I don't know how I would've reacted if you'd told me the first night we met. Maybe I would've cared. Maybe I wouldn't have. We'll never know. But I know I never would've treated you like a whore, and now I have to work my way out from underneath finding this out from someone else. I have to deal with knowing you lied."

"I didn't lie," Rory said, trying to fix things. "When you asked what I do, I told you I was in the entertainment industry and about my graphic design. When you didn't dig, I didn't offer more."

"And you think that makes this okay?" Kentucky didn't yell. In fact, he sounded downright calm. "You think it's okay to keep something like this from someone you're building a relationship with? You introduced me to those guys, knowing I was clueless. Betrayed doesn't begin to cover how I feel right now."

All Rory had was this one chance to try to hang on to Kentucky. He knew if he couldn't find the right words tonight, he'd never hear from him again. "Look, I know it's hard to wrap your head around this if you've never done what I do, but Jay, Lucas, Shawn, and Bryson, they are my friends and nothing more. It's a job, and that's it. You're the only man in my head. They would never disrespect you."

"Great. So you don't care if I hit the bar tonight, find some random dude, and fuck him? As long as he doesn't touch my heart, it's no big deal. Is that what I'm hearing?"

Rory's eyes fell closed. Kentucky was no different from anyone else. Jay had been right. It was best he stuck with his circle of people. No one else got it, and he shouldn't expect more. He stood. "Thank you for being a really fantastic guy. There should be more men like you in the world." He had to get out before he lost his shit. Rory could feel the pressure building in his chest, crawling upward and ready to burst from him in painful waves. "I'm sorry you can't say the same for me. I won't bother you again."

Kentucky shifted to his feet. His fingers encircled Rory's wrist, stopping him from running away. He looked genuinely hurt. The knowledge did nothing to help Rory's growing despair. "Give me time to think, okay? I just need a minute to absorb all this and figure out if it's something I can handle, okay? Stop," he said when Rory swallowed hard. Tears pressed at the backs of his eyes. "Stop," Kentucky repeated, hauling Rory against his chest. It was his undoing. Kentucky was so warm and big. He was like coming home to the most comfortable and safe place. It was hell knowing he wouldn't get to do this again. Kentucky was too nice. He wouldn't want Rory again. Rory already knew he'd never hear from the man after tonight. He couldn't stop swallowing and fighting back tears. Kentucky stroked his back. "Shhh. I don't think you're a bad person. This just caught me off guard." His lips brushed Rory's temple. "Fuck. You really do just fit perfectly in my arms." His hold tightened on Rory. "It's like a punch to the throat, knowing I have no shot of having you to myself."

"You already do," Rory said, speaking through the burn. "I just don't know how to convince you that you're the only man I want. It hurts that I have to convince you." A single hot tear fell from Rory's lashes. He swore it singed his skin as it rolled down his cheek. His fingers found Kentucky's shirt. He held on, desperate to keep him. "I'm so sorry. Every time I tried to find the words to tell you, they wouldn't come." In a burst of Herculean strength, he pried his fingers away from Kentucky's shirt and took a step back. Rory swiped at his eyes. No matter how hard he tried, his gaze wouldn't lift to meet Kentucky's stare. "It was really nice getting to know you. Don't give up your hunt for a team." Rory headed for where he'd left his shoes by the door. If

Kentucky said anything else, Rory didn't hear it. His ears rang and his mind raced. It seemed like he probably had stuff he was leaving behind. None of it mattered in the face of losing Kentucky. He didn't know if it was worse or better, knowing it was all his fault. As he headed for his car, he decided it didn't matter. Either way, he'd lost a part of himself. Rory hadn't thought he had another piece of his soul to spare.

He drove home on auto-pilot through a haze of tears. After he parked, he stared at nothing for so long, his windows fogged over. Rory had no clue how much time passed before he finally made his way inside. He bypassed his bedroom and headed up the stairs. Rory was scared of what would happen if he went to bed alone. Maybe he wouldn't wake up. The pains in his chest didn't bode well for survival. He opened Lucas and Jay's bedroom door without knocking. No one ever knocked in their house. Boundaries had disappeared so long ago between them, Rory didn't remember what privacy looked like.

Rory toed off his shoes and stripped down to his underwear before crawling into the bed with the couple. He didn't even look to see whose side of the bed he chose. Lucas lifted the covers and tucked

Rory against him. Neither of them spoke. They didn't have to. They'd grown up inside the same group home. It was like they could read each other's mind. Feel each other's pain. Lucas kissed his temple. Tears dripped from Rory's eyes onto the pillow. Tomorrow, he'd harden his heart. He'd pick himself up and return to being alone. The only people who'd ever loved him lived under this roof. Rory would do good to remember that in the future and stop wanting more. When his mom had abandoned him at eight at a fire station, she'd taught him the one harsh truth he needed. He was unlovable. Cursed from birth. Rory's choices were to live with it or die from it. Sometimes, it was a close call.

SIX

EVERY SOUND INSIDE THE SHOP POUNDED AT Kentucky's brain. His head throbbed. The pain had nothing on the one happening inside his chest. The Mustang in bay four had already taken him forty-five minutes longer than he anticipated. If he could focus, he'd have its owner on their way. Instead of seeing the inconveniently placed spark plugs he should be focusing on, Rory filled Kentucky's head. He'd left his phone at Kentucky's house in his rush to leave Saturday night. Kentucky wondered if he'd made it home okay. It had taken every ounce of his self-control not to drive over and check. He could return Rory's phone as an excuse, but then again, he couldn't. His sanity couldn't take it. The runner-up for testing his willpower was searching Rory's name. Kentucky had fought with himself all of Sunday. Several times, he'd typed Rory's name into his search engine, needing to know how bad it was. Each and every time, he'd deleted his search before hitting enter. It was bad enough knowing the truth without seeing it.

"Do you want to come to dinner tonight? Bring Rory."

Kentucky kept his gaze locked on his hands at his dad's question. Not only did he need to get this car finished, he didn't want his dad to see his reaction. "I don't think so. Rory and I are on a break, I think."

Brad moved closer and lowered his voice for them alone. "Do you want to talk about it?"

Kentucky shook his head. "Not really. I'm still working things out in my head, and I don't want to say anything you might hold against him later. For all I know, I'll get over this."

"Is this about the porn thing?"

Kentucky's mouth fell open. His gaze snapped to his dad's face. "You know about that?"

His dad shrugged. "Your mom recognized him right away."

That was more info than Kentucky had ever

wanted to know. "Great. Even my mom has seen him in action."

Brad snorted. "I never took you for a prude."

The accusation stung. "I'm not. This isn't about that. What if you found out Mom fucked other people behind your back for money?"

"How much money we talking?"

He was serious. Kentucky was blown away. "I can't believe you're serious right now. Are you telling me it wouldn't bother you?"

Brad shrugged again. "I don't know. It's never happened, but if we were in a horrible position and Lexi might starve, I wouldn't hate her for doing what she needed to keep us afloat. You don't know what led to those decisions." His dad looked one hundred percent positive he was in the right. Kentucky couldn't stop hanging on every word. "You heard what Rory said at Lexi's party. He doesn't have a family. Only a group of friends who are like family. Not everyone is given the opportunities you were." Brad leaned his hip against the car and held Kentucky's stare. "If you don't think you can live with his choices, that's fine. You shouldn't have to if that's not what you want, but don't judge him for things you don't understand. It's been nice to see you happy. You haven't been in a long time. Even when you laughed, there was a sadness to it. Hell, I thought when you got picked up by New York, you'd be over the moon, but no." His dad shook his head. "You were still missing something. Since you met Rory, that's changed. Now, even when you're upset, it hasn't taken the light from your eyes. Don't walk away from that without some deep soul searching. You won't find someone like Rory around every corner, and we like seeing you smile." Brad slapped Kentucky's shoulder and moved away. "Plus, Rory offered to keep Lexi for us this weekend so we can hit the beach. Don't fuck that up for us."

"Betrayed by my own parents," Kentucky muttered.

Brad didn't look the least bit ashamed. "Don't introduce us to someone nice if you don't want us to like him." He nodded toward the car. "Once you finish that up, why don't you head out. Take some time to figure out your life."

Kentucky nodded and forced himself to focus. He needed to get out of there and get to where he'd be free to think. Once he figured out his feelings, he'd be better either way. The uncertainty of the situation was killing him. It wasn't just the porn thing. That was bad, but there was something else eating at him that he couldn't nail down. He wanted to scream. The frustration and unhappiness; they were choking him.

He finally got the car back together and to its owner. With a nod in his dad's direction to let him know he was out, Kentucky headed for his truck. Once inside, he didn't feel better. Kentucky didn't bother listening to music on the way home. His head was too full. Over and over, he sifted through every word and conversation. A few things kept rising to the surface. Rory hadn't lied. He might not have told him the exact projects he worked on, but Kentucky hadn't asked. One hundred percent, Rory should've told him anyhow, but Kentucky hadn't asked. That bothered him more than it should. It was like, since meeting Rory, Kentucky had soaked up the man's attention. Rory's complete focus on him was so addictive that Kentucky hadn't realized he'd sat back and let it happen. What kind of shitty, selfish boyfriend didn't ask any questions? Kentucky didn't think he'd even once asked Rory how his day had been. Hundreds of incidents came to mind when he should've peppered Rory with questions. Instead, he'd sat back and soaked up all the constant ego stroking. He'd never thought of himself as a bad person. When he looked back on his time with Rory, he wondered why Rory wanted him at all.

Another issue that wouldn't stop eating at his mind was along the same lines. As his dad had pointed out, Kentucky didn't know what led Rory to those decisions. Not really. Rory had made it sound as if it was just a way to pay to stay in California. But Kentucky remembered Rory's face the day he'd said he'd been raised in a group home. Now Kentucky had a million questions he should've asked already. What happened when he turned eighteen? Did he get turned out with nothing? Kentucky's chest ached. If so, how did he eat? Where did he sleep? Kentucky couldn't imagine being a kid and having no one. No money. No place to go. His dad was right. In the same position, a person would do what they had to do to survive. Maybe Kentucky would've known all those things sooner if he'd asked.

By the time Kentucky made it home and took a long shower, he still hadn't gotten any closer to knowing what to do. He scrolled through his phone, looking through all their texts. Every crazy picture Rory had sent him had him pausing to stare. A smile pulled at his lips at the image of Rory with dog ears from one of those online filters. He missed Rory. It had only been two days since he'd last seen him, and the separation was killing Kentucky.

He needed to focus on something else for a

while. Clear his head. He needed to feel the ice beneath his skates. Once the thought hit, Kentucky didn't hesitate. He grabbed his stuff and headed for the local rink. It wasn't until he was on the ice that he realized he hadn't come for the ice at all. This was their first date. Under this roof, he'd experienced his first spark of interest in anything or anyone in years. Everything had been muted before that night. Kentucky had been focused on his career and the loss of it for so long, he didn't care about anything else. Then, he'd stopped to zip Lexi's jacket and Rory had skated in, stealing him away from the darkness he'd lived in for too long. That was another thing his dad had been right about. Kentucky hadn't been happy. When he'd been picked up by New York, he should've been elated. In fact, he'd gone through the motions of elation because it seemed he should, but no. He hadn't been happy back then. There'd always been something missing.

He skated to the short wall separating the ice from the game room. As Kentucky stayed out of the way of other skaters, he lost himself in the discovery. After Rory skated into his life, Kentucky had taken him home. Rory had fallen asleep in his arms. Kentucky had stared down at him, and Rory's question about what Kentucky wanted with his future had eaten away at him. He'd been so goddamn happy in that moment, he'd thought he'd figured things out. Kentucky had felt then the way he should've felt getting picked up by New York. But it hadn't been hockey that gave him that feeling of complete elation. It was having Rory in his arms. It was being asked what he wanted to do with his life by someone who genuinely cared what he wanted. Most of all, it was having Rory look at him with complete faith and solidarity in whatever decision he made—like he'd still be there no matter what Kentucky chose. That was what had filled him to completion.

Kentucky dug out his phone and scrolled through his contacts until he found the number he needed. His call was answered on the third ring.

"Hello?"

"Hey, Kieran. It's Kentucky."

"I didn't expect to hear from you so soon." Kieran's cool tone didn't give away his thoughts on the matter. His tone was always cool. "Have you already come to a decision?"

Kentucky gave a short nod, even though Kieran couldn't see him. "Tell Mississippi I'm not interested."

When Kieran spoke, Kentucky could hear the

smile in his voice. "Good. I'll keep hunting for a team with better terms."

"Thank you, but I'm not interested in that either. I've got something better going on here."

Kieran chuckled. "I hope by that you mean Rory. It's not my business, but you won't find someone who looks at you the way he does every day. It's obvious he thinks God broke the mold when he made you."

Kentucky couldn't stop the smile that stretched his lips. "Yeah, I mean Rory. For the first time, I don't want to chase after some unattainable dream. I feel like I already have it here."

"That's good," Kieran said, sounding like he meant it. "You're a very lucky man. After seeing the way he watches you, I honestly believe he'll never stop trying to make you feel like you're the only man on the planet for him. That's a good place to be. I found that in Henley and can truthfully say it's made for an amazing life. It doesn't matter what your career is as long as you're together at the end of the day."

Kentucky knew Kieran meant his career, but Kentucky heard it like he meant Rory's. He found himself nodding along. Rory came home to him. More than once, he'd shunned the world to be alone with Kentucky. He couldn't lose that. Just as his dad and Kieran had pointed out, Kentucky wouldn't find someone else who treated him the way Rory did. Kentucky didn't deserve him.

"Thank you, Kieran. For everything, seriously. I know if you don't find me a team, you don't make any money on me. I feel like I've wasted your time."

"You probably won't believe this, but I'm a sucker for love." Kieran sounded serious. Kentucky believed. "More than once, I've gone for a lower commission to keep a player with their other half. Rory loves you. I'd feel guilty forever if I helped take you away. Go have a good life, but don't lose my number. Next time you call to meet, you can bring Rory to dinner with us or something. Mia would love to see him, I'm sure."

"You have a deal."

Kentucky's smile didn't abate until he slipped his phone back in his pocket. A horrible thought sneaked in. He wasn't the only one who'd had time to think. Maybe Rory wouldn't want him back after the way he'd reacted. He couldn't imagine how he'd feel if Rory had flipped out after learning he'd played hockey, treating him like he'd probably fucked a million fans while on the road. Damn. He might've already ruined things. At the realization, Kentucky was out of his skates and in his truck in record time.

He probably needed a plan, but he didn't have one. Still, as he pulled into Rory's driveway, calm settled over him. The peace he'd been searching out for the past two days was right here. Even though Kentucky wasn't sure of his welcome, he didn't hesitate to ring the doorbell. He held his breath and waited.

Jay answered, looking less than thrilled to see him. "Kentucky."

The way the man said his name didn't give Kentucky the warm and fuzzies. "Is Rory home?"

For a solid minute, Jay eyed him. He looked ready to slam the door in Kentucky's face. Instead, he sighed. "Come in." He walked away, leaving the door standing open.

Kentucky slipped inside. The house was quiet. Just as he'd been the first time he been there, Kentucky was blown away by the opulence of the place. Everything was marble and light. Open and bright. The place looked like royalty lived there. It didn't appear anyone else was home. Kentucky followed Jay to the main room.

Jay spoke over his shoulder as he headed for the off-white and plush couch. "When we lived in L.A., I met a guy like you," Jay said, sounding sad. "He wasn't in the industry, but I fell for him so hard. I was scared as hell to tell him how I make my living." Jay sat and met Kentucky's stare. His eyes were a sweet brown. He looked innocent and younger than his thirty years. "One day when I came home, he was sitting on my bed and watching one of my movies." The life left Jay's eyes as he spoke. "A chill raced up my spine. I'd never been scared of him before that moment. But there was something in his eyes." Jay shook his head as if shaking off the memory. His flawless features turned cold. "After he beat me and raped me, he spit on me and called me a whore. He said there wasn't a court that would convict him because no one cared about sluts. He was right. I spent two weeks in the hospital and another month in bed. He got three months' probation. We had to move here just so I could feel a little safe again." Jay's voice turned hard, but it was nothing compared to his eyes. Kentucky felt sick. Jay didn't stop. "Don't take it personally, but fuck your feelings. Rory had every right to fear your reaction. If you're here to hurt him, you won't leave here. I won't make the same mistake twice, thinking the courts will handle it."

That was fair enough. Jay had a right to his rage. "I would never hurt Rory." Kentucky shrugged and shook his head. "I love him. It was a blow to find out from someone else, but it doesn't change the way I feel. Is he here?"

Jay nodded toward Rory's closed bedroom door. "He's in there, working."

Kentucky hesitated at the claim.

Jay rolled his eyes. "On his graphic design stuff, idiot."

As much as Kentucky wanted to take umbrage over the insult, it already looked like it would be a while before he got back in Jay's good graces. He gave Jay a nod of thanks and headed for Rory's room. Kentucky quietly opened Rory's door. If Rory was busy, he didn't want to disturb him. Instead, he spotted Rory on the bed. His hands were cupped beneath his face. He slept peacefully, looking almost like a small child curled up in a ball. His laptop was open on the bed. With a sigh, Kentucky closed the door behind him. It was dangerous to leave a laptop like that. Kentucky picked it up to move it before it overheated and caught the bed on fire. The screen woke, showing him a half-finished image of a Pegasus. It was gorgeous work. With a smile, he set the laptop on the nearby desk and moved back to the bed. For a moment, he watched Rory sleep. Damn, the man always hit him in the chest with his beauty. He couldn't wake him. It didn't feel right. Instead, he circled the bed and climbed in behind him. When he scooted in as close as possible, Rory cuddled against him in his sleep. The backs of Kentucky's eyes burned as their bodies molded. He couldn't imagine living without this. They still needed to talk, but Kentucky didn't want to lose this man who'd stolen him. When it came down to a choice between what he could live with and what he couldn't live without, the decision was easy. Rory had ruined him for anyone else.

A SOLID WEIGHT across his waist had Rory pinned to the bed. He slowly rolled. The vision of Kentucky sleeping beside him had Rory's throat swelling. He'd never seen a more beautiful sight. As much as Rory wanted to wake him and find out why he'd come, Rory couldn't stop staring. He wondered how long Kentucky had been there. Rory had no clue of the time. Since leaving Kentucky's house that final time, he hadn't slept at all until he'd fallen over in exhaustion while working. One hour or twelve could've passed since then. Rory had cried so much in the past couple of days, he wasn't even a hundred percent sure what day it was. All he knew was he was dehydrated but hadn't cared enough about himself to get anything to drink. It seemed nothing mattered without Kentucky.

"Do you hate me?" Kentucky asked the question without ever opening his eyes.

The burning was back behind Rory's eyes, but there wasn't enough moisture left in his body to cry. "No. I hate me." Even to his ears, Rory sounded hoarse.

Kentucky's gorgeous blue eyes opened. "Are you sick?"

Rory didn't respond. Hell would freeze before he admitted to crying himself hoarse. In a way, he was sick. Sick at heart. Sick of life.

"Have you checked to see if you have a fever?"

Rory still couldn't find his voice to answer.

Kentucky didn't give up. "When was the last time you had anything to eat or drink?"

"When I cooked for you Saturday night."

The way Kentucky's eyebrows rose made Rory wonder again what day it was. "Don't move." Kentucky rolled from the bed and disappeared. Since Rory was too exhausted to move, Kentucky's order wasn't hard to follow. He wanted to be happy Kentucky was there, but he might only have shown to let Rory know they were over for good. That was the most likely scenario. In truth, Rory would've preferred Kentucky do it over the phone, but he'd left his phone at Kentucky's house in his rush to get away. He'd also left behind a bag of clothes and all his toiletries. The only thing he still had in his bathroom was his toothbrush, because he already had one of those at Kentucky's house, and a tube of toothpaste, because he always used Kentucky's. Rory imagined he probably stank. Not that he cared. Losing everything didn't hurt any less when he was clean.

Kentucky reappeared with a bottle of water in hand. "Come on," he said, urging Rory to sit up. "Let's get this water in you."

Rory reluctantly accepted. His arms felt weak as he lifted the bottle to his lips. Maybe he was getting sick. Kentucky wouldn't let him stop until the bottle was empty. He felt a little better. Mostly, he couldn't stop staring at Kentucky. He was gorgeous. This might be the last time Rory got to sit and look at him.

His stomach rolled. The room spun. Nope. No. He didn't feel better. Without warning, Rory leaned over the edge of the bed and puked out the water. Part of him was thankful that was all he had in his stomach. That is, until the dry heaves hit.

"Damn, you're burning up," Kentucky said while rubbing his back.

Rory tried to catch his breath. "Well, this is humiliating." Rory buried his head beneath his pillow and prayed for death. Now that he'd experienced the first symptoms, the misery of truly being sick slammed into him.

"It's okay, baby. I've been there. Don't move. I'll be right back."

Kentucky's cool touch disappeared. He thought he might've dozed again because Kentucky was right back like he'd never left. He tugged on Rory, forcing him to sit up.

"You can go back to sleep in a minute. First, we need to do some things. Take these pills and sip the water this time. Hopefully, you can keep them down."

Everything had a dark hue—like he'd pass out at any moment. Rory still did as told. His stomach didn't heave this time, but the water felt terrible sitting on his gut.

"Lucas will help you strip him and I'll run him a cool bath," Jay said to Kentucky, sounding like he came from a distance.

"All my stuff is at Kentucky's." Even to Rory's ears, he sounded weak.

Jay snorted. "Think about where you live, queen. We've got you covered."

Lucas and Kentucky flanked him on either side, tugging at his clothes. He was helpless to do anything other than watch.

"I hope you're okay with this," Lucas said quietly to Kentucky as if Rory wasn't the one losing his clothes.

"It's fine." Kentucky's voice sounded tight.

Lucas didn't let up. "Rory and I grew up in the same group home together. I was already there when he showed up when he was eight. We've taken care of each other like this during illnesses dozens of times. There was no one else."

Kentucky paused in stripping Rory to meet Lucas' gaze. "I'm not worried over you helping me. My only concern is his health. He's dehydrated."

"Y'all are so sweet." Rory's voice slurred. He couldn't control it.

"We'll make him better," Lucas said, ignoring Rory's fevered talk. From that point, everything turned into a blur. Then, there was nothing.

KENTUCKY WAS beyond impressed with Rory's

friends. Even once Rory passed out, they still managed to get him bathed. They patted Rory awake several times during the process, forcing water into him. No aspect of his care was missed. They even ensured Rory had on deodorant before dressing him again. Kentucky didn't think he had a single friend like them. If he got sick, he'd have to just lie in it until he could clean himself. As that thought passed through his mind, he remembered the way Rory had cared for him after tryouts. Maybe he had one person like them. Even though they didn't have to, each of Rory's friends asked his permission before doing anything to Rory's person. He thought they had more rights than he did, but he still appreciated their show of respect to their relationship.

After they had Rory back in bed and Shawn mopped up the mess, Lucas and Kentucky were left alone with Rory. Lucas occupied the chair at the desk, while Kentucky sat on the bed, stroking Rory's hair. They sat in silence for several minutes before Lucas made a move as if to leave. Kentucky stopped him.

"So you two were in the same group home. How old were you when Rory arrived?"

Lucas sat back down. "I was nine."

"Did you live there your whole life?" Kentucky

knew he was being nosy, but he should've been asking more questions before now.

Lucas nodded. "Pretty much. I was six when I got there and stayed until I turned eighteen."

"I thought they didn't put kids under twelve in group homes." Kentucky heard the horror in his voice, but he couldn't stop.

"They didn't pass that law until it was too late to help us. Not that it matters. You're no more prepared for that life at twelve than six." He nodded toward Rory. "But we had each other."

Kentucky wanted to know everything. Since Rory wasn't awake to answer, he went for the next best person. "What happened when you left?"

Lucas seemed more than willing to answer any questions Kentucky had. "I went to work on an oil rig for six months, making a fuck-ton of money killing myself, while Rory applied for emancipation. As soon as Rory was free and finished school, because I wouldn't let him leave town before then, we took the money I'd saved and split. We made friends and crashed with whoever would let us stay. When we met Jay, everything changed. We went from never having anything to this," he said, motioning to their surroundings. "More than that, he ensured we didn't have to depend on the charity of others. He not only shared what he had but made sure we had it for ourselves. I know you're upset with Rory, but sometimes people can't afford to care what others think. We weren't given the luxury of pride."

"I'm not upset," Kentucky said, correcting Lucas' assumption. "Obviously, I was at first. I needed time to think."

Lucas eyed him, expressionless. "And now?"

Kentucky made a helpless gesture. "It seems being with him is more important to me than anything else."

"That's good to know," Lucas said, coming to his feet. "Rory is very tender-hearted. He gets lonely easily. He's the kind of person who needs hugs and feels the loss if he doesn't have them. It doesn't take much to crush him. He needs someone strong but loving. From the beginning, I've thought you fit the bill. I hope you prove me right." He headed for the door. "If you need me, just yell. I'll come back later and check on you."

Kentucky nodded. "Thank you." Once Lucas left him alone with Rory, Kentucky snaked his hand beneath the blankets and felt of Rory's skin. It was still hot but not on fire like it had been. Kentucky sent a quick text to his dad, letting him know Rory was sick and he wouldn't be in to work for a couple of days. With that out of the way, he settled down beside Rory. "I won't let you be lonely." He stared at the way Rory's eyelashes fanned across his flushed cheeks until sleep pulled him under. Kentucky would keep the promise Rory didn't know he'd made.

SEVEN

The next time Kentucky opened his eyes, Rory was staring at him without blinking. Kentucky's heart raced into his throat. "Are you okay?"

Rory nodded, and Kentucky's heart slowed. "I thought I'd dreamed you were here, and I was scared to open my eyes."

He still sounded like shit and his face was flushed. Kentucky felt of his forehead. "You're still burning up."

"Yeah. I'm not feeling great."

Kentucky sat up. "You just said you were okay."

"I am."

Kentucky blew out a sigh. It was like Rory didn't think he mattered at all to anyone. "Hold that thought while I grab you some more meds and water."

Rory didn't make a sound. Kentucky made a quick trip to the bathroom before heading for the kitchen. He was quickly learning his way around. After grabbing two bottles of water from the giant stainless-steel fridge, he found the medicine shelf Lucas had shown him earlier. With everything in hand, he headed back for the room. Voices floated from Rory's open door. Kentucky's steps slowed. It wasn't his intention to eavesdrop. That didn't stop him from trying to hear every word after hearing his name.

"Kentucky is here taking care of you. That's got to have you already halfway on the mend."

When Rory spoke, it sounded like it ripped out his vocal cords to rasp out each word. "Don't get your hopes up. You're the only person who's ever cared about me. I imagine you're the only person who ever will, and we'll never love each other that way. It's okay. Maybe I should head back to California. You're with Jay now and Bryson and Shawn have given up pretending Shawn hasn't moved into Bryson's room. I'm just in the way."

"You could never be in the way," Lucas argued.

"I can't imagine not seeing your face every day. We swore to always take care of each other."

Silence dragged on so long, guilt sneaked in for listening. Kentucky tensed, ready to make his presence known when Rory spoke again. "My soul is tired, baby. I feel like I'm a hundred years old. In California, I can disappear."

"What do you mean?" It was like Lucas took the words from Kentucky's mouth.

"You know what I mean."

That was it. Kentucky stepped through the doorway. "I don't."

Lucas' gaze shot to the door. He looked slightly guilty for some reason. Rory didn't look his way.

Kentucky walked to the edge of the bed and stared down at him, refusing to be ignored. "I don't understand what you mean."

"I'll leave the two of you alone. Let me know if you need anything." Lucas practically ran from the room. Kentucky couldn't say he blamed him.

Rory's gaze slid Kentucky's way before sliding away again. Damn. Rory looked like he felt awful. Kentucky didn't have the heart to interrogate him.

"Come on," Kentucky said, helping Rory to sit up enough to drink some water and take a couple of pills.

Rory stared at his lap and toyed with the covers between sips. He looked younger than ever. Broken. Kentucky couldn't take it. He set the water aside and wrapped his arms around Rory.

Rory didn't hug him back. "Stop. I don't want to get you sick."

"Hush. I want to hold you. It's been like three days and my heart hurts. Jesus, you're hot. I think I should take you to the doctor."

Rory's arms lifted as if he thought to hold Kentucky. They fell like he expected to be rejected. "Don't worry over me."

"It's my job to worry over you. What would you do if I was the one who was sick?"

"I'd do whatever it took to make you better."

Kentucky urged Rory onto his back. "That settles it. Rest for a minute. I'll be back." He went in search of Lucas. Thankfully, he was sitting on the couch. "Does Rory have a regular doctor he sees, or do I need to take him to a walk-in clinic?"

Lucas looked up from the book in his hands. "He has a doctor. I'll find you the number."

With a nod of thanks, Kentucky got moving. First, he called the doctor. Luckily, they had an open appointment. With that out of the way, Kentucky dug through Rory's clothes, finding him something that matched. He'd noticed that seemed to matter to Rory. Rory was in and out as Kentucky dressed him. He found socks and shoes. The shoes halfway matched his outfit too. Kentucky patted himself on the back over that one as he tied Rory's shoes. Finally, he wrapped Rory in a blanket. Even though it was eighty-six and sunny, Rory had a high fever. He didn't want him to get cold. With Rory ready to go, Kentucky rushed through getting himself ready too. After ensuring he had everything he needed, Kentucky scooped Rory from the bed and headed for the door. Lucas spotted him and rushed ahead of him, opening the door to the house and truck for him. Kentucky buckled Rory in. His concern notched up by the second. Rory was too quiet and more asleep than awake.

Lucas looked worried too. "Let me program my number in your phone. That way, you can keep me posted."

With a nod, Kentucky unlocked his phone and passed it over. Thankfully, Lucas was quick. Kentucky was ready to go. At the doctor's office, Rory was a little more lucid. He walked into the building under his own power. Mostly. Kentucky refused to let him walk without Kentucky holding on to him. The wait felt like forever. He knew it had to feel twice as long to Rory. No one liked sitting at the doctor's office when they felt like death. Rory wasn't holding up as well by the time they made it to a room.

"Relax," Kentucky said, urging Rory onto his back while they waited.

Rory shook. "I'm cold. Why can't I just go back home? I feel too bad for this."

Kentucky shamelessly dug through the cabinets until he found a stack of sheets. He grabbed two and covered Rory. "It's almost over. I'll make you better."

A dark-haired doctor came through the door. "Hello, Rory. I'd ask how you're feeling, but that would be crazy." He checked the screen of the small laptop he carried. "Hmmm. One hundred and three fever. That's not good. We're not really into flu season yet, but I still want to test you for it. It's not unheard of for cases to start showing up this early."

Rory didn't respond. He stayed still and let everything happen to him. The doctor swabbed Rory's nose and throat.

"I'll be back in a few minutes."

Once they were alone again, Kentucky went

back to trying to keep Rory warm. The seconds ticked by, stretching Kentucky's nerves. He bit back a sigh of relief when the doctor reappeared. "Well, his strep test came back negative. Unfortunately, the flu test was positive. I'm going to write a prescription that should cut the length of the virus in half." He focused on Kentucky. "I take it you'll be the one caring for him."

Kentucky nodded.

"I'll write a prescription for you too. Go ahead and start taking it right away. That way, if you get it too, it shouldn't be anywhere near as bad."

"Okay." Kentucky couldn't get sick. Rory needed him.

The doctor kept talking, keeping Kentucky from spewing his thoughts. "Rotate between Tylenol and Ibuprofen every four hours. Rest and stay hydrated. If he gets worse or his temperature gets higher, go to the emergency room."

"I've got him." Kentucky meant every word. He wouldn't leave Rory's side.

With prescriptions in hand, Kentucky helped Rory back to the truck, lifting him inside so he didn't have to climb. Once again, he buckled Rory's seatbelt for him before wrapping him in the blanket. Rory's teeth chattered, making Kentucky's heart squeeze. He needed to get Rory back in bed.

The second he was behind the wheel, he shot a quick text to Lucas, letting him know his plans.

Kentucky: *It's Kentucky. Rory has the flu. I'll take him to my place so he doesn't get anyone there sick. You might want to sanitize the house.*

Lucas: *Poor thing. Keep me posted and text me if you need anything. I'll scrub his room.*

Kentucky: *Thanks.*

With that out of the way, Kentucky headed out to control what he could. His heart didn't stop pounding until he had a bottle of water and meds in Rory. The worrying had him exhausted. When he tucked Rory beneath the covers, he climbed in with him. He held Rory tight, uncaring of the flu, the heat, or the shaking. They were a team. They were in this together.

"You have to get better," Kentucky whispered against Rory's temple. "I have so much to say."

To his surprise, Rory gripped his shirt in a surprisingly strong hold. "Don't disappear. Everyone I love disappears."

Kentucky held Rory tighter. Considering how slurred Rory's voice sounded, Kentucky didn't think he'd remember this moment. Kentucky would never forget. He couldn't imagine the scar it would leave to be discarded at a young age by his mother. Rory had to have some horrible abandonment issues. The other thing stealing Kentucky's breath was the fact that Rory had confessed to loving him. He didn't know how to react. Part of him was ecstatic to know he wasn't alone in his feelings. Another part of him quietly broke over the realization of how much pain Rory hid behind his constant smile. Kentucky would make it better. He would be the one person in Rory's life who never left. Kentucky had the strength Rory needed.

RORY WOKE UP ALONE. It took him a minute to figure out where he was. When he realized he was in Kentucky's bed, he sat up. For once, his head didn't spin. The last thing he remembered with any clarity was puking on his bedroom floor. He half-ass recalled going to the doctor—like it happened in a dream. A bad dream. One where he felt awful and was freezing. Rory dropped his feet to the floor. He half expected to not be able to walk. Weakness weighed down on him, but his head was clear. Rory pushed to his feet. His body didn't fail him. As he caught sight of himself in the bathroom mirror, Rory hissed. There were dark circles under his eyes, his hair was a matted mess, and a week's worth of growth covered his chin. He hoped like hell Kentucky hadn't looked at him while taking care of him. His current appearance almost rivaled the humiliation of puking in the floor.

Rory didn't even think about it. He climbed into the shower. No way could he go on living in his own filth. The hot water felt amazing on his skin. He popped open his body wash and inhaled. There was nothing better than being clean. He took a longer than necessary shower, standing under the water until he felt halfway human. Rory wrapped himself in a fluffy towel and dug through the drawers until he found a comfortable outfit. He wasn't ready for style yet. Once he was dressed and in front of the mirror once more, Rory's brain took a different turn as he brushed his teeth. He was inside Kentucky's space again. After the last time he'd been there, Rory had told himself he would leave the man in peace. It wasn't fair for Rory to be here. Kentucky deserved to be free of him. Somewhere out there was an amazing man, waiting for Kentucky to find him. Someone who wouldn't lie or steal his opportunities. Kentucky should already be signed with a new team. If not for Rory, he would be.

Rory stared at himself in the mirror. People would always recognize him. He would never be anything but an embarrassment to Kentucky. If it only affected him, Rory didn't give a fuck what anyone thought. He wasn't ashamed. But when it came to everything he'd stolen from Kentucky, he was filled with regret. Kentucky was the greatest guy. He deserved the world. Rory should set him free. It was the humane thing to do.

While holding tight to that thought, he headed for the closet and found his overnight bag. His gaze swept the bathroom. The idea of packing left him exhausted. Rory sat on the edge of the bathtub and looked around again. He didn't know where to start. They'd only been together a couple of months, but their lives were already so entwined. Rory had bottles of crap in the shower. His toothbrush was in the toothbrush holder. There were bottles of different products scattered across the vanity. He knew there were a few things in the cabinet. Rory thought he even had some stuff under the sink.

He stood and tossed his empty bag back in the closet before heading back out to the bedroom. The dark blue curtains blocked out most of the sunlight, but there was still enough to see. Between that and the light spilling out from the bathroom, he could make out the whole room. The king-sized bed had a built-in bookcase in the headboard. There was a book resting on Rory's side. It was his. There was also a bottle of lotion there that belonged to Rory. Three of the drawers in the oak chest of drawers were Rory's now.

With a new realization dawning, he opened the bedroom door and stepped into the living room. His phone and laptop were on the coffee table. He didn't know how his computer had gotten there, but there it was. His shoes were by the door. More than one pair. Rory headed for the kitchen. His gaze landed on his coffee cup, hanging on a hook above the coffeemaker. Kentucky had bought it for him because Rory liked the funny saying on it. It was from one of his favorite movies.

Rory's gaze moved to the stove. Kentucky stood there cooking with his back to Rory. Rory eyed his wide shoulders and perfect ass. All that was his too. His new realization settled into his chest. He fucking lived here. Maybe not full-time, but Rory—at some point in time—had moved in, and Kentucky had let it happen. How the fuck had that happened? Rory didn't care. He wouldn't give this up without a fight.

Maybe he didn't deserve Kentucky, but he could change that. Rory closed the distance between them. He wrapped his arms around Kentucky's waist and pressed his lips to the spot between the man's shoulder blades. If Kentucky wanted him gone, he'd have to shove him away and toss him out. Rory wasn't strong enough to walk away.

"Oh no. I'd planned to bring you breakfast in bed."

The backs of Rory's eyes burned at the claim. "It's not too late. I could get back in bed." Gah. His voice still sounded horrible.

Kentucky set his spatula aside and turned in Rory's arms. He cupped Rory's face while his gaze moved over Rory's features, looking concerned. "Maybe you should. You still don't sound one hundred percent."

"I'm good. A little tired and weak, but I feel a lot better. I needed to get up and shower. Hell, I don't even know what day it is." He felt stupid having to ask, but everything had been a blur since he'd left here last.

Kentucky held him and stroked the small of his back. "It's Saturday. You've been in and out all week."

Horror overcame Rory. He'd been down longer

than he thought. "Oh no. I was supposed to keep Lexi this weekend."

"Don't worry about it. As soon as Mom heard you were sick, she added Lexi to their reservation. He went with them. I figured once you were better, I'd surprise them with another weekend getaway and we'd keep Lexi that weekend instead."

Kentucky talked like they had a future. Like he wasn't done. "Okay." Another thought hit. "Damn. You missed an entire week of work because of me. First, I let your mom down and then I left your dad shorthanded. Great." Even to Rory's ears, he sounded despondent. He'd been failing everyone right and left lately.

"Nope. Don't worry about Dad." He tilted Rory's chin up, forcing Rory to meet his stare. "Don't. Okay? Dad sent me home on Monday and told me to straighten out my life. He was tired of watching me mope. Even if he hadn't, he wouldn't have blamed you for getting sick. If Mom had been sick, he would've been the one out. He knows it's my job to take care of you, and he expects it of me. That's how he raised me. Family first."

"I'm not family." Fuck. Rory couldn't stop the pitiful-sounding words from falling from his lips.

Kentucky's features softened. "You are, because

you're everything to me. If you can't tell by now that I love you, I don't know how else to show you."

Rory blinked. He wasn't sure he'd heard correctly. "Did you just say you love me?"

Kentucky blew out a sigh. With a twist, he turned off the stove and moved the pan from the eye. "Come on. That voice of yours really does still sound horrible. I don't think you should be up yet." Before Rory could argue, Kentucky swept him off his feet. All Rory could do was hold the man's neck while Kentucky carried him back to bed. After settling Rory into his spot, Kentucky climbed into bed next to him and gathered Rory against his chest. He stroked Rory's hair, making Rory's eyes fall closed. "Bryson stopped by earlier. He brought some more of your stuff. Another bag of clothes and your laptop. He says you have a deadline, and he didn't think you'd want to miss it."

Rory nodded but kept his eyes shut. He couldn't stop soaking up the attention. "I'm almost finished. It'll get done on time. You didn't answer my question."

"That's because I realized something important when you left me. You're always the one who asks the questions." Kentucky brushed Rory's hair away from his face, stroking him and making Rory want to cuddle closer. "Why don't you answer a question for me? Were you happy with me? I mean, before everything went wrong."

Rory nodded. "I never wanted to be anywhere else. When you invited me here that first night, I felt like I'd won the lottery. I never wanted you to look at me the way you did when Kieran told you everything. That's no excuse for not telling you, but I knew it would hurt every bit as much as it did."

Kentucky didn't look away or back down from the topic. "You should've had a little more faith in me. I know I let you down with my initial reaction, but do you know what I wholeheartedly believe?"

Rory couldn't stop hanging on Kentucky's every word. He looked at peace. Rory wanted to feel that way too. "What?"

Kentucky touched Rory's jaw, ensuring he didn't look away. "In my heart, I honest to god believe if you'd stayed that night, I would've been over it by morning. That's how much I love you. I can't see myself without you." Kentucky blinked as if the words hurt. When he spoke again, his voice came out in a whisper. "I need to know you can't see yourself without me."

"I knew who you were the first time we met."

Confusion etched Kentucky's features. "Okay."

"I didn't tell you I recognized you because I didn't want you to think I was some crazed fan. That's what I would've thought. I also don't want you to think I'm keeping anything else from you."

Kentucky's confusion didn't clear. "Okay."

Rory didn't let up. "Because I love you and I can't see myself without you." Rory touched Kentucky's cheek. He needed to feel the man beneath his palm.

Kentucky turned his head and kissed Rory's wrist. With his eyes closed, he kept his lips pressed to Rory's skin. He took a deep breath as if inhaling Rory's scent. "Please don't leave me again," he breathed against Rory's skin.

"I didn't want you to see me fall apart. It killed me knowing I'd hurt you. It's not an excuse, but I think I sort of hoped you just didn't want me to know you'd heard of me."

He felt Kentucky smile against his wrist. His eyes shone with laughter when he met Rory's gaze again. "Nope. You should probably take my man card. I don't watch porn. Obviously, I have. A really long time ago. It wasn't for me."

The fact that Kentucky was openly discussing the topic kept Rory talking. "Hold that thought." He rolled from the bed and raced to the living room.

After grabbing his laptop, he returned to the bed. Rory fired the device to life. While Rory waited for everything to load, he explained his thoughts. "I don't think you'd completely hate everything I've done." He pulled up some images and turned the screen Kentucky's way. "See."

RORY'S "SEE" was all the warning Kentucky got before he was staring at the hottest fucking picture he'd ever seen in his life. It looked like a magazine spread. In a sexy pose and hard as steel, Rory was on full display. Kentucky found himself moving closer to the screen. He tried to be practical. "Is this a magazine?"

Rory nodded. "It's part of a spread I did for a skin magazine. I've done a few of those." He clicked around on the computer. "Here's something else you might not hate." A video popped up on the screen. It was Rory on a white couch. A perfect backdrop for his caramel skin. He stroked his cock, looking turned on and ready to blow. Kentucky went hard, disproving his earlier words about porn. The thing was—it was Rory. He was sexy and mind blowing. He belonged to Kentucky. Kentucky couldn't look away. He could watch Rory all night. Kentucky imagined countless people felt the same way, and it was his bed Rory shared. Rory loved him. Goddamn. He was a lucky bastard.

Rory shook his head. "It doesn't feel real when I see myself like this," he said, sounding pragmatic, considering how turned on Kentucky was beside him. "I can't tell you how long it took me to get comfortable doing things like this with tons of people standing around."

Kentucky leaned closer to the screen as if he could peek around the edge to see the people for himself. "There are people there?"

Rory's chuckle sounded deeper than usual with his fucked-up voice. "Who do you think is recording me? There's a cameraman and a ton of other people milling around off screen. They're eating breakfast and scrolling through social media on their phones. The typical viewer sees me while I see a bunch of people at work on a Tuesday. If that's not an erection killer, I don't know what is." Rory's shoulder lifted in a half shrug. "Anyhow, that's me. That's how I made my money." He shut the laptop, stealing the vision from Kentucky.

Kentucky tore his hungry gaze away from the closed device that hid Rory's hotness. He had the real thing in his bed. "You're beautiful and make me proud," Kentucky said as he shifted to his knees. He set the laptop on the headboard before covering Rory's body with his. "I still prefer the real thing."

Rory stared up at him, looking stunned. "I make you proud?"

Kentucky nodded. "Life handed you nothing, and you didn't let it beat you. You survived and found me. Goddamn, I'm proud you didn't give up."

The way Rory blinked as if fighting tears let Kentucky know he was right. Rory had thought about giving up more than once. "I love you." Rory's voice came out in a whisper.

"I love you too." Kentucky placed a light kiss on Rory's chin. "How are you feeling, seriously?"

A small smile passed over Rory's lips. "Like I just had the flu, and it wiped me out."

"What do you need to make it better?" Kentucky really needed Rory better.

"Can you just cuddle with me for a little while?" Rory's question sounded so vulnerable, Kentucky's heart twisted.

"Come here, baby," Kentucky said, shifting positions. With a roll, he tucked Rory against his chest. Face to face, Kentucky rubbed Rory's back, doing his best to bring him comfort.

Rory buried his face against Kentucky's neck. Every few seconds, his lips would brush Kentucky's throat. The gentle caress had Kentucky hard as a rock. He kept enough space between them Rory wouldn't notice. Kentucky didn't want him to think this was about sex. He just wanted to make Rory happy.

"I knew you'd be at the ice rink when I accidentally on purpose ran into you."

A smile tugged at Kentucky's lips at the quietly spoken confession. "I know. The lady who works the front counter, Anna, she told me after you left the shop that day that the two of you had been talking about me. She said she'd told you where I'd be in passing and it didn't occur to her until afterward that you might be a crazy person. Since I was already worried I'd missed my chance, I hoped you'd show."

A chuckle vibrated against Kentucky's throat, making the erection problem worse. Rory took a deep breath. His chest expanded at the move. As he released the air, it blew across Kentucky's skin, causing goosebumps to rise. "There's still a part of me that's scared shitless we're not okay."

Kentucky drew back where he could see Rory's face. "Why?"

Rory shrugged. His gaze skirted away. "You

won't kiss me. I mean, you kissed my chin, but it's like you—"

Kentucky touched his lips to Rory's, cutting off whatever stupid thing he was about to say before it could make him crazy. As always, the moment their tongues brushed, an explosion of desire burned through Kentucky. Without thought, he had Rory underneath him again. He rocked against the man automatically, seeking relief. This was why he hadn't kissed Rory. It had nothing to do with not being okay. Rory still wasn't a hundred percent and Kentucky didn't know how to hold back with Rory. He needed Rory too much. Loved him too much. Kentucky tried pulling back when he couldn't control his body's reaction. "I'm sorry. You're still—"

Rory held tight, refusing to let him pull away. "Make love to me," he said, killing Kentucky's argument while it still lingered on his lips. A devilish glint flashed in Rory's eyes. "Of course, you'll have to do all the work since I'm short on energy, so if you don't think you're up to the challenge…"

Kentucky didn't argue. Instead, he slowly stripped their clothes while stealing kisses and touches. "You're so beautiful."

"Thank you."

Kentucky smiled at the sweetness in Rory's

voice. "On the inside too," he added, dipping his chin and touching his lips to Rory's. "You won't be sorry for keeping me." As he made the claim, Kentucky boldly stroked Rory's erection. Rory sucked in a hiss. Kentucky couldn't help trying for more. He massaged Rory's balls and fingered his ass while kissing him deep. Rory's hips lifted, seeking more as delicious moans came from his throat, vibrating around their entwined tongues.

Kentucky blindly reached for the lube and a condom. Pre-cum dripped onto Rory's stomach and Kentucky's hands shook in his need as he fumbled around trying to suit up. His brain itched like he hadn't been inside Rory in years. He couldn't explain why Rory always made him this way. Kentucky always went from zero to ready to blow the moment they touched. With a condom in place, Kentucky tried to slow down. His lubed fingers fucked Rory's ass while Kentucky tried focusing on their kiss rather than his weeping cock. Damn, he loved the way Rory's full bottom lip felt between his teeth. He liked where those lips felt other places too. One night while they'd cooked, Rory unexpectedly dropped to his knees in the kitchen while waiting for water to boil. Kentucky's chin had hit his chest. Rory's lips had locked around Kentucky's dick and he'd blown in Rory's mouth before the first bubble appeared in the water. He'd never experienced anything like it. His orgasm had been hard and fast while the suction hadn't let up.

At the memory, Kentucky pushed inside Rory. He pumped at the man's cock like it was his as he impaled Rory. The tight heat squeezing him had Kentucky sucking in a hiss. He leaned away and held Rory's stare. The flush on Rory's cheeks and the way he sucked air through slightly parted lips nearly stole Kentucky's orgasm right then. He held still and concentrated on giving Rory the world's best hand job while the sensation passed.

"You make it hard for me to last long enough to please you. It's never been like this for me."

A soft moan escaped Rory. That was all the warning he gave before cum jetted through the air, coating his skin. That was all the permission Kentucky needed. He reclaimed Rory's lips, biting his lips before delving deep. He sucked Rory's tongue as he pounded inside him, reaching as his body wound tighter. The pressure building in his cock had him gasping. His lungs stopped working for half a heartbeat. Pleasure exploded through him, causing his heart to skip several beats. His hips kept moving, seeking every last pulse. Kentucky rolled to his side as he collapsed, bringing Rory with him. Their lips clung. Each of them refused to give up their kiss. In that moment, Kentucky believed nothing could tear them apart. They were strong and meant to be. Rory was that thing he'd been missing for years. His other half.

EIGHT

Four months later...

While leaning against the short wall separating the ice from the game room, Kentucky zipped his jacket. Kieran leaned against the opposite side of the wall while they watched their men skate. Even though it was almost sixty-five degrees outside, the local ice rink always kept their building freezing freaking cold. He could handle it, but he felt bad for Mia and Lexi. They both were sporting red noses. Kentucky knew he should skate over and steal Rory away. He'd yet to give the man his birthday present, but he enjoyed watching him too much. Plus, he didn't get to see Kieran often. He liked spending time with him.

"Are you sure I can't interest you in returning to

hockey?" Kieran asked, cutting into Kentucky's ever-growing plan to steal Rory from the party.

He focused on Kieran. "Yep. I kind of like being home every night."

Kieran nodded. "I just thought I'd ask. Your old team contacted me, saying they'd love to have you back if you're interested in returning. It's local. You wouldn't even have to move. Not to mention, they already know you and wouldn't care about Rory."

Kentucky nodded. Even though he'd been grinding, trying to make it to the majors the entire time he'd played for Houston, he had liked playing for the Ice Devils. The coaches were great, and the owner was hands-off. Still, he loved seeing Rory's face every night. "I'll think about it." Kieran's offer brought up another point that had been eating at Kentucky. "How did the owner of the Jackson team know I was dating Rory?"

Kieran looked amused. "Don't you ever search your name online?"

Kentucky felt his face screw up in confusion. "Why would I search myself? That seems vain."

Kieran pulled out his phone and shook his head. He typed while he talked. "I know you're not actively looking for a team, but you should always stay on top of what's being said about you online.

You can bet your ass teams are keeping an eye on your private life. Here." He passed his phone to Kentucky.

Kentucky stared at the device in awe. There was a picture of him kissing Rory before skating onto the ice before tryouts. "Porn sensation Rory Vega AKA Young Houston seen kissing hockey star Kentucky Armhill. Ha. Damn. They got a good picture too. Impressive."

A chuckle escaped Kieran as he put his phone away. "Yeah. These people are sneaky." Kieran looked around. "This was a cute idea, by the way, throwing Rory a birthday party at an ice rink. He looks like he's having a blast."

Kentucky followed Kieran's gaze to where Rory and Henley were helping Lexi and Mia skate. Kieran's daughter wore the tiniest pair of ice skates Kentucky had ever seen. In truth, she wasn't truly skating on her own at all. Rory was doing all the work. "Rory didn't get anything like this growing up. This might be ridiculous for anyone else his age, but it's perfect for him."

"You two make a great couple. How's living together going? You look happy."

Kentucky couldn't stop smiling. "We've pretty much lived together from day one. Finding a place for Rory's furniture was really just a formality, but it's been great."

"I'm glad things worked out. However, I do feel as if I should shake you for stealing Rory from the rest of us. Henley and I love his movies."

Kentucky had expected remarks like that to bother him. They didn't. "Don't blame me. I didn't have anything to do with the decision. I told him I'd love him no matter what. How's it going with Mia?" Kentucky asked, changing the subject. "It looks like she's come out of her shell a bit."

A small smile hovered on Kieran's lips. It was odd to see him so relaxed. "I never saw myself as a parent, but I could see Henley as one. The minute he started talking about adopting, I had to make it happen, but I never expected to enjoy it beyond seeing Henley happy. Then Mia showed up. She's ours. I can't imagine life without her and I never thought I'd love someone so much."

Henley and Rory skated over. Mia sat perched on Henley's forearm, but she threw herself forward as soon as she spotted Kieran. Kieran plucked her from Henley's hold and accepted her kiss.

"That's so sweet," Rory cooed before stealing a kiss from Kentucky. "Your mom took Lexi to play video games. Lucas promised to take her out on the ice later. She's over the moon."

Kentucky nodded and shamelessly stole another kiss from Rory. "You'd make a great dad. Always worrying about everyone else," he said between kisses, completely understanding what Kieran meant. He'd do anything to keep Rory happy.

Rory snorted and playfully pushed him away. "I'm too selfish. I like having you to myself too much."

Henley laughed. "I used to say all the same things. You should definitely get married first, though. Equal parental rights, having both names on the papers, and all that."

Even though Kentucky could tell Henley was joking by the laughter in his eyes, there was nothing Kentucky wanted more than to know Rory was tied to him for life. Kentucky checked Rory's reaction. Rory turned away but not before Kentucky caught the longing etching his features. The one thing Rory didn't have that Kentucky could give him was a family.

"We should."

Rory glanced over and met his gaze. "What?"

Kentucky smiled. "We should get married." He

could tell by Rory's smile the man was gearing up to blow off his suggestion. Kentucky held out the ring he'd been holding, waiting for the moment he could steal Rory away. Now the moment felt right—witnesses and all. "I'm being serious. You should marry me." Kentucky could feel several sets of eyes upon him. If he got shot down, it would be a very public display, but Kentucky wouldn't stop trying until Rory said yes.

Rory's gaze moved from the ring to Kentucky's face. His eyes were wide. "You're really serious—like you have a ring and everything."

Kentucky nodded. "I've just been waiting to get you alone."

"We're not alone," Rory said, pointing out the obvious.

Kentucky shrugged. "I don't care."

"Say yes," Kentucky's mom yelled from twenty feet away, making him realize exactly how many people were watching.

Rory leapt, nearly knocking Kentucky off his feet as Rory climbed him, kissing Kentucky's face every place he could reach. "Yes."

Several people were laughing at Rory's antics, but the lump in Kentucky's throat wouldn't let him make a sound. Rory's feet slipped back to the ground as their lips met. "I love you," Kentucky choked out against the man's lips.

Rory pulled away just far enough to slip the ring on before he was back to kissing Kentucky. Kentucky stroked Rory's back and pulled away. "I love that you're this excited and you haven't even gotten your present from me yet."

A line appeared between Rory's eyes. "This wasn't my present?"

"I wouldn't cop out on you like that," Kentucky said, slightly offended. "If I'd done that and you had said no, you wouldn't have had a gift."

Rory rolled his eyes. "You know full well I wouldn't have said no."

Actually, Kentucky hadn't known that at all, but it was good to hear. "I'm taking you to New Orleans for a week to celebrate your birthday." Without glancing behind him to check if they were still there, Kentucky motioned Kieran and Henley's way. "These guys are going to show us all the best hotspots."

Rory dropped his voice to a whisper. "Can we get married while we're there? I don't want a big wedding."

Kentucky shrugged. "If you'd like, but you'll break my mom's heart."

"Fuck." Rory looked crestfallen. "You're right. Jay would die too. He loves a good wedding." For a moment, Rory held his stare in silence. Sometimes, it was like they didn't need words to let the other know they loved each other. "I'll make a great husband."

Kentucky nodded. "I know." He did too. If Kentucky knew nothing else, he knew spending his life with Rory would be the best thing ever. Like his dad had once pointed out, even when Kentucky was upset with Rory, he was still happier with Rory than he'd ever been in his life. They'd found that forever love. Kentucky would treasure Rory until his dying breath.

Keep an eye out for more "Hard Hit" books.

Please consider leaving a review at the retailer where this book was purchased. Reviews really help with a book's visibility, which ensures I can continue writing. Thank you, Charity.

ABOUT THE AUTHOR

Charity Parkerson is an award winning and multi-published author with several companies. Born with no filter from her brain to her mouth, she decided to take this odd quirk and insert it in her characters.

*Seven-time Readers' Favorite Award Winner
    *2015 Passionate Plume Award Finalist
    *2013 Reviewers' Choice Award Winner
    *2012 ARRA Finalist for Favorite Paranormal Romance
    *Five-time winner of The Mistress of the Darkpath

Connect with her online:

--Join my street team: facebook.com/TeamCharityParkerson
    --Sign up for my newsletter: http://bit.ly/CharityNews
    --Website: charityparkerson.com

--Facebook:
facebook.com/authorCharityParkerson
facebook.com/TheMenofSin
--Twitter: twitter.com/CharityParkerso